1

5:15 AM. Dash was late again. I'd been waiting about thirty minutes for him to pick me up, and trust me when I say that waiting outside the strip club on any given night in Atlanta isn't the safest thing to do. While he took his sweet time, I could've been mugged by now and he would still pull up with a shrug and a half-hearted excuse. It wasn't like he was sleeping. Dash didn't sleep during the night. But then again, the sun *was* coming up soon.

All of the other girls already left. The DJ and the clean-up crew had all been long gone. I was hungry, sleepy, body aching – the works. I just needed his two-toned Hellcat to pull up so I could relieve my bladder and find the solace of my bed at home. It was too early for the Indian grocery mart to open and the gas station across the street had too many roaming bums, so I just had to hold it for now. I tried not to pace around too much but I still stuck out under the single plaza light like a pretty thumb.

It was useless to try calling again. My calls were going straight to voicemail for the last hour. I was sitting on my duffel bag, tapping my feet on the concrete, when finally the steel blue and black car came creeping around the corner, music blasting. He pulled up in front of me and the door locks clicked. When I sat inside, he turned the music down and asked me, "You ate?" I shook my head. "Want anything? Waffle House? Mcdonalds? I want a egg and sausage biscuit, myself."

Still, I said nothing, just locked my eyes on the passenger window.

"You got a fucking problem, shawdy?"

"I don't know who you're talking to like that. But just so you know, yes. I have a problem because I got off over an hour ago and you don't pick up the damn phone. I have to pee so bad I can't focus on being hungry. And I'm so sleepy I just wanna skip going to the bathroom so I can lie down. Damn right I got an attitude."

"Shawd' you know damn well you get off at different times depending on the night. How the hell am I supposed to know."

"Keep your damn phone on and stop sending me to voicemail and you'll know. I almost called a fucking Uber. But nah. My ass, worried 'bout you, didn't wanna not be here when you pulled up if you were already on the way. Can we just go?"

"I ain't having this argument with you this early in the morning. Get ya attitude together, man."

I rolled my eyes and he turned the music back up. The conversation was closed. He pulled into McDonalds and made his order. I didn't ask for anything, but he still got me a hash brown and a plain sausage biscuit. I was so upset that I refused to receive the bag when he tried to hand it to me. I couldn't even *imagine* taking one sip of the sweet tea he ordered. My bladder was on fire. I should've asked him to pull up so I could go inside and release, but I had no words for him. He always made it seem like I was making a big deal out of nothing. I hated that shit.

We pulled up in front of my apartment and he turned the music down again when I reached for the door handle. He popped the locks and took my wrist.

"Dash. I'm sleepy."

"When you gon' quit this shit, shawd'?"

"When I start to show. Why it matter to you?"

"*Why does it matter?* 'Cuz I already told you I got you. You don't need to be up in that bitch with all that smoke and shit in the air."

"Well, I don't smoke, so it don't even matter." That was a partial lie.

"Second hand. You know what I mean."

"Dash, just the inside of this car smells like a pound. The hell are you talkin' bout? I'm sleepy. We can talk later. I'll call you when I wake up. I might need you to take me to Kroger..."

"Yeah."

I got my shit and went upstairs.

I woke up later around two in the afternoon. Didn't get to sleep as long as I wanted, but I knew I had things to do. I wasn't feeling sick for a change. Usually all of that smoke and alcohol breath had me feeling woozy for a few hours after my shift. My nose had become extremely sensitive. I didn't want to admit it, but Dash had a point about that atmosphere. No place for a woman to be while two months pregnant, but I was serious about paying my own bills. Dash always stressed that he could do it all for me, but he was flaky enough. He worked on his time and his time only and I was not comfortable with that. Not in my situation. Besides, our relationship barely survived the last stupid stunt he pulled and probably wouldn't have if I didn't realize that I'm pregnant. So what did I look like putting my whole life in his control? With him, it wasn't no telling.

After I took a shower, I rolled half of a bidi and smoked it quickly. I sprayed as much febreze as I could stand just in case he showed up and wanted to come inside, and then I sat down to count my money. I texted him in the meanwhile and asked him if he was busy. He told me he would come by in the next hour to take me where I needed to go.

Depending on Dash to get around the city was getting annoying, fast. He never followed his word when he named a time. He always came hours late to get me. My car was in the shop because the transmission was out. With all the money I was making, I was conflicted on whether to get my old Saturn fixed or junk it and just get another used car. My car was raggedy as crap and I would feel better pushing a new whip, but facing reality, it would be wise to just stick with what I had and avoid monthly car notes. I had to save up with this baby on the way.

I separated my cash and put up the access. I didn't have a bank account. I kept all my money in a container in my room. No one but my sister knew what was in the box. I hid it in plain sight just so that I wouldn't forget where the hell it was, and I could always keep an eye on it that way.

An hour later, Dash still wasn't at my place. I was ready to be outside when he called. I was laid up in jeans and a Led Zeppelin cropped tee. When my phone rang, it was my best friend Kaycee instead of Dash. I answered the phone with a disappointed sigh. "Hey."

"Tonnie! You know you was supposed to call me earlier around twelve, right. Thought you wanted me to redo your hair today?"

"Shit, you already at work huh? I completely forgot. It can wait 'til another day. It's not that bad. I just need a touch up cuz I already sweat my silk press the hell out. At worst you know I'll rock a ponytail until it's dead."

"It's cool. I was feeling a lil lazy anyway. Shit, I didn't even remember we had an appointment 'til after I got here to the shop."

Kaycee did hair professionally and was nice as hell with the razor. Her styles and designs were amazing, long lasting, and natural looking. So many people believed these 22-inch i-tips I had in was my real hair. Instead of going to the shop, though, she did my hair at her house because she never charged me full price and the shop she worked at wasn't hers.

"Well, next time then. It doesn't look bad. It's just something I notice. My leave out areas is growing out. I can feel it."

"Mm Hmm. How was last night? Was it good?"

"I mean, for a Wednesday night, yeah. I made over two stacks. You know who was there. So…not bad."

"True. Well, I'm jugglin' about three heads in this chair. I was just callin' cuz it seem like we both forgot. I gotcha tomorrow, though. I'll call in the morning and give you a little time to sleep."

"Alright, girl. Later."

Kaycee was cool. She's been my homegirl since the tenth grade. She was younger than me, but sometimes I felt like she was ashamed of me. Okay, maybe ashamed wasn't the right word to use. I felt like she thought I was beneath her. She has always been a real smart girl, real stylish, and she went to cosmetology school and made a living that way. Every now and then she'd make it seem like I wasn't serious about life because I never went to school for anything. We just had different opinions. Dancing worked for me, and I was never behind on bills. That's all that mattered.

Speaking of being behind, I'd heard Kroger had a sale on steamed crab legs this week and this nigga still hadn't called. I tried calling him. Got his voicemail. I cussed at him and put the phone down, went into the kitchen and got some Doritos to snack on, trying my best to fool my mind into tasting Old Bay seasoning. I guessed it was going to take a while. All I could do was hope and pray they wouldn't be out of crab legs by the

time he finally showed up. Trying to fool my tastebuds wasn't working, and the more I waited and snacked, the more pissed off I became.

My family crossed my mind so I called my mother, but apparently she'd left her cell at home. I settled for talking to my stepdad for a few minutes. I didn't really like him when I was younger but I realized that I wasn't the easiest kid to take care of, especially considering how fast I was back then. So now in my adult years I was constantly trying to strengthen our relationship. After speaking to my stepfather, I texted my sister. I already knew her enough to know she never answered the phone, but she was a text junkie. She was probably in class, anyway.

I switched the Doritos out for a bag of salt and vinegar chips, plucked one out, then put it back in the bag and rolled it closed. Just by the smell I knew I wasn't in the mood for that like I thought I was. Pregnancy was making me a picky eater. That's how I knew to go get a test. It seemed like nothing I ate was ever enough, but I couldn't eat just anything. And my craving for ice. I had a craving for ice by the first month and speaking of ice, I could go for a nice cool cup of it. I got up for the cup and opened the freezer, but had to put the cup right back down as soon as I put the first cube in. The Roddy Rich song he told me to set as his ringtone played from the other room. I rushed back around the doorway to get my phone off of the couch. Dash was finally calling.

2

She walked that fine ass down the steps in some tight ass jeans. I damn near pulled at my dick by the sight of her. I was heated to think about how that body was about to be ruined. Her surgeon did his fucking thing cuz swear, she had the most perfect BBL I ever seen. The shirt she had on showed her waistline and some of that tattoo that made me stupid, the one that started on her thigh and ran all the way up her side and over her left chest. Her skin shined under the sun. It was obvious to even me, as a man, that her pregnancy glow was in full effect.

She came to the car door, swung it open with attitude and sat down, crossing her arms over her chest immediately.

"Yo, what's ya' problem now?"

"Nothing, Dash. Nothing at all. Just take me where I need to go. Store, please."

"You trippin', shawdy."

She kissed her teeth and looked out the window. I wasn't moving the car any-fucking-where until she fixed her constant attitude. Her moods were crazy and I didn't understand it.

"You say you're coming to pick me up at two, and here you are at four-thirty. How you know I didn't have any other plans? I always gotta run shit on your clock and I'm getting so tired of the bullshit. You finally pull up when I was 'bout to make a fucking cup of ice, and now that you finally come, I still want my fucking ice."

"Where the ice, then? Go get the fucking ice."

I put the car in park. She rolled her eyes and got out. I stopped fronting and watched that fluffy ass go back up the stairs. Shit, she had a nigga stupid for her, man. I wasn't happy about a new baby, but Tonnie was *my* baby. I left all the groupie hoes alone, even this other stripper bitch I used to mess with. I used to think she was the baddest chick in the game until I met Tonnie. Tonnie had it locked down ever since. She had my son's mother jealous as hell. I wanted to do everything possible to make her happy and keep her satisfied with whatever she needed since she was pregnant and all, but I had to be real careful to make sure she didn't think that she ran a nigga on a puppet string just because she was carrying my seed. Half the time I wasn't really mad at her, I just had to get extra spicy on a bitch to let her know she wasn't about to nut up on me for any damn reason. I was the man. She was the female. That was the bottom line.

Tonnie came back down with a Styrofoam cup full of ice and slammed my car door shut.

"Watch ya'self, shawd'. You already know I don't play when it comes to my fucking car."

"Yeah, we all know your car is priority. Can we go now?"

"Yo' smart ass fuckin' mouth, I swear."

"Whatever." She pushed it every time but I let her get the last word.

After I took her to the store she asked me to go pick up her sister. It wasn't a problem. I had other things to do anyway, so I didn't mind dropping them off back at Tonnie's. One thing I didn't appreciate was her sister's bad ass attitude. Shit was *worse* than Tonnie, but at least I was smashing Tonnie, feel me. Her sister and I never liked each other from the first time we met, and not like I gave a shit, but how you gonna be all up in my damn car and don't even have the home training to speak? I'd call her on that shit if she was anyone else, but if I said something and Ginger happened to snap back, Tonnie would get involved with her two cents, and then I'd be outnumbered. So I left it alone.

Once we were back at her place, I caught Tonnie's wrist as she got out the car the way I usually did when I had something to say. "I'ma come back through later on, aight?"

"If you say so, Dash."

"Nah, I'm for real. Just let me run to the studio right quick and I'll be back over. See you later, shawd'."

"The studio is never 'right quick'."

Her sister was already standing outside the car rolling her eyes impatiently so I just let Tonnie go and drove off. Women had to be so fucking difficult. But, the studio was only a partial truth. I had pampers and wipes in the trunk to drop at my baby momma's house for our two-year-old before I went to go handle some business. Tonnie and her sister's fucking attitudes brought mine down and that was all bad if I was going to go meet with Shakima. Shakima never made it easy to come around.

I got a few calls about some green and some hard on the way out to Stone Mountain, so that would have to be handled too before I arrived at the studio. Hopefully I could make this visit quick so I could get to my money. If God was with me, Shakima wouldn't be on the same bullshit today.

When I pulled up, an unfamiliar car was already in her driveway parked behind her Kia Sport. I ain't really like the way that looked, but I went up and rang the doorbell anyway with a bulk box of Huggies under my arm. I felt like she was playing me cuz I had just called and told her I was pulling up, and yet I was still standing outside the door at least a minute after I rang the doorbell. I knocked instead, and by the fifth knock, it swung open. I stepped back so she could open the screen door.

"Who's that?" A man's voice came over her shoulder and for a second it sounded like a motherfucker had a problem.

"Dash here." She called back to whoever it was and turned to me with a smirk.

"Whatever the fuck you think you doin', it ain't working, but a nigga don't need to know I'm here by name and shit. I don't have to report my attendance or ask nobody permission to come around, so if you gonna tell him who's here tell him it's a nigga at the door that'll pop his fuckin' cap back." I handed over the box and she took it, rolling her eyes.

"Was all that really necessary?" she asked.

"What you think? Where's my son?"

"So it's a nigga here and now you care 'bout where ya son is?"

I gave her the straight face. "Shakima don't bullshit with me. Don't be having my son around all them no good niggas, man. And you betta not be letting some broke nigga discipline my fuckin' son. Just get that straight. Just in case."

"Sure, you right. Look, when I need help around here, you don't be around. I'll handle my business the way I'm doing, however I want."

"You talkin' to me like my son isn't my business and you tryna flex like I didn't just come out here with that big ass box of pampers. Little man is two years old, anyway. Why the fuck isn't he potty trained?"

Shakima held back laughter. "At two? Huh, shows how much you know about children." She sighed deep and adjusted her robe. "Well, nigga, if you was here handling business you'd be able to teach him how to use a damn toilet but since I don't get any help, it takes a while for me to get around to some things. You talk a lot of shit about my parenting from someone who's never here because you want to go be with that stripper bitch. Buying pampers don't make you no type of father. Fuck you, Dash."

"He still here? Is there a problem?" The face to match the voice appeared into view from the kitchen. Some scrawny looking young nigga in a beater and some basketball shorts. No shoes, no socks. Looking real fucking comfortable like he was trying to claim territory. Sometimes young niggas didn't know any better. He was flexin' on the wrong one.

"Ay nigga, I don't know what you think this is, but you don't want it with me. You have a problem? Can Kima talk at the fucking door with her son's father without you being all in her ass? Grown folks is talkin'."

Shakima turned around to face him. He looked like he didn't know what to say, but he was still pissed. No doubt about that. I didn't give a shit.

"Roger, don't mind my ignorant ass baby daddy. I'm cool. Thank you, babe."

I laughed. "Roger, huh? You betta check Roger and let him know to sit his country ass down."

"Thanks for the fucking Huggies."

She slammed the door in my face, and instead of being mad, I was actually happy that this meeting was finished. I turned for my whip and pulled out my phone, ready to get to my business for the night.

3

I liked being over at my sister's place because this guy I was dealing with stayed out on her side in Clarkston. He didn't have a car either, and I got around by MARTA, so being here made things easier when it came to seeing each other. I didn't exactly love Tonnie's neighborhood, but she'd lived on this side for years and nothing crazy had ever happened. That calmed me.

Tonnie texted me earlier and asked if I wanted to come hang out and eat crab legs, so I decided to kill two birds with one stone. She'd met Kenny before and she liked him, so the three of us sat up in her apartment watching Hulu, cracking crabs over junk mail magazines and coupon pages until someone knocked at the door.

"Want me to get it?" Kenny offered. He was a nice dude like that. His momma had raised him with manners. He was really quick to hold doors and pump gas for a woman, even a female stranger, and I loved that. He didn't treat it like a sign of weakness and I didn't look at it as one. There needed to be more guys around like him. From the way he behaved, you could tell he wasn't from here. He was just here as a student at Georgia State but his people lived in Savannah. We met last semester at a Kappa probate out there on his campus and we'd been vibing ever since.

Kenny looked through the peephole and turned to my sister. "It's ya dude."

She nodded and gave him permission to let Dash in, the same time I rolled my eyes and got ready to witness the slack ass treatment my sister settled for. And to know she was about to bear a child for his stupid ass. The thought made my stomach hurt. He was so lame to me. Fuck his illicit money. He had nothing going for him and had nothing to offer a child for future reference. Just to know how he handled his existing baby's mother, I wondered what the hell made Tonnie think that she would be the exception once a few years passed by. But I was just the little sister. I couldn't tell her anything.

Dash came in and dapped up Kenny, then took a seat next to Tonnie aside her rolling food tray. I sighed, sitting there on the floor, and held my face up with my hand dramatically. Kenny nudged me and begged with his eyes for me to be polite. I looked at him and shrugged.

"Hey, shawdy."

"What's up. Didn't take you long."

"I told you so, shawd'. You ready for work?"

"Maybe in another hour. I'm full and tired."

"Don't you gotta pay more when you go in after midnight?"

"Who cares? You paying my tip-in?"

"Damn, calm down. Just a fucking question."

The way he spoke to her crept under my skin with claws. Kenny would *never*.

"Kenny, you wanna come sit outside with me for a second?"

One look at me and without anything further he nodded, stood from the coffee table and helped me up. I couldn't sit in that room anymore and listen to Dash spit his obscenities at Tonnie so carelessly. Once the front door closed behind us, we took a seat on the steps and I breathed in the humid air, relieved. Rain was coming.

"I couldn't sit there another second. He already started the bulslhit."

"I heard. I don't understand how a man could mistreat a woman like that when she's about to give him a child. Don't that nigga have a mother somewhere?"

"Exactly what I'm saying. No home training."

It was quiet for a few seconds as we watched cars pass ahead.

"You know the OVO tour is coming out here next week? You tryna go?"

"I heard it was sold out already. You plan on trying to get tickets?"

"Maybe."

"I'd go, but I know for certain they said it already sold out. Either that or we gonna be up in Phillips Arena in the nosebleed section," I laughed.

"It won't be a problem. So you trying to go or not?"

"Uh…yeah. If I can, why not."

"Well then I hope fifth row sounds good. I couldn't get first row."

"Kenny? Floor seats! For real? Where did you get tickets from?"

"Don't worry about all of that. But just don't stand me up. It's a date."

I leaned back and looked at him with the serious face. His smile was too confident to deny. "Well hell yeah! I'm there. You don't have to worry about that. I can't believe you have tickets. That's great! I love Drake."

"I know."

"Kenny. What did you do? I mean, how? Fifth row had to run about a few racks….where'd you get that type of money to spend on a Drake concert?"

"Damn, babe don't worry. We got tickets and that's all you gotta know. We're gonna have fun. That's it."

"Wow. You good for this one. I'm not asking anymore questions." So silence hit again. Not awkward silence, but thinking silence. "When do you think you'll be ready to settle down, Kenny?"

He turned to me with scared eyes. I laughed. "No, silly. I'm not saying it like that. I mean, I'm just thinking about how my sister is short-changing herself just because she's getting older…or just because dude has money. But I think she can do so much better. He's a grown man with no plans to ever settle. Just from a guy's point of view I just want to know when guys think it's good to calm down and just give one person the attention they deserve. Or is that impossible to ever ask of a nigga?"

He shook his head and ran a hand down his chin. "Well, I don't think you ever have to worry about ending up like your sister because for one, your standards are a lot higher. What you think is right is not impossible. A man should always handle his business. Even if he's not ready. You get yourself into a situation, you should be man enough to deal with it."

"So what about you? What's your future plans looking like?"

"Well, soon as I finish school I wanna move out of Georgia. I'm done with this state. I've been here long enough to understand it's not a lot here for me. It's much more outside and beyond whatever Georgia has to offer. Maybe California...I don't know about kids but maybe early 30s...late 20s....marriage? Probably around the same time, I guess."

I nodded. "Good. Take your time, Kenny. You'll make a wife really happy."

He scooted closer. "You're so sure it won't be you, huh?"

I smirked, but became too nervous to look at him. Not many guys have ever accomplished the feat of making me blush. Not many could make me feel all fluttery inside. He was talented.

"Um...I'm not saying that. I mean, it's just a lot of years between now and then. You can never be sure."

"Uhhh huh." He smiled and nudged me by the shoulder. "C'mon walk down to the gas station with me. I want some snacks."

While walking down the street, he caught my hand and locked it in his, and my heart flip flopped in my chest. It would be a blessing to know Kenny until we were thirty. It would be too good to be true to mix genes with his and push out a beautiful little baby. His features were gorgeous. He told me his dad was West African and his lips were the evidence. I *loved* his lips. His eyes on the other hand, were a very European gray, and his hair was a thick, Cuban curly. Neither he nor I could guess where the hair came from. But his opal black skin was the killer. I loved it more than anything else about his appearance. Silly, brainwashed girls turned away from his blue black skin, but it shined so pretty when the sun hit, and the contrast from his eyes melted me. In my opinion, Kenny was an undiscovered model. I wouldn't mind having gorgeous, dark-chocolate children with him.

All of that, *plus* he's studying to become an architectural engineer. Intelligence is a *heavy* turn on for me.

Kenny said he wanted snacks, but when we got inside the AM/PM, he got two cheese dogs and a soda. He offered me the entire gas station, and I laughed at that, but all I asked for was a bag of Teddy Grahams, a Fanta, and some sunflower seeds.

We got back to my sister's apartment just as she was bringing her bags down the stairs.

"Ginger, I'm going to work. You and Kenny going to be cool or do you need Dash to drop ya'll off somewhere else? I don't mind leaving you with the keys."

I looked at Kenny and hesitated. I wouldn't mind having alone time with my sweetheart for once. Only thing was, we both had class in the morning. "Kenny, what do you wanna do? I got my MARTA pass so I'm cool with it."

"I can get home same way I came, by Uber Feets."

I rolled my eyes and tried to hide how much his corny joke had me swooning and nodded at Tonnie. "Pass me the keys. We'll behave."

"Girl, I don't give half a shit. Here. Come get the keys. My hands full."

"Why Dash ain't helping you with your bags? Where that nigga at?" I asked while tossing the house keys to Kenny.

Tonnie sighed. "Don't start, Ginger. He upstairs takin' a piss or something."

"You should've waited for him to help you. Give me the one on your back. This is stupid. He know you shouldn't be trying to carry all this heavy shit. You got his car keys?"

She shrugged. "Just wait, Ginger. Put it on the car."

Kenny was halfway upstairs with the keys I handed him when Dash was coming down. "You tryna wash the car, Ginger?"

Tonnie answered before I could get anything out. "Shut up, Dash. It's just a damn bag."

I took a harsh breath. "Tonnie. I'll be in the house. Have a good night at work." She shook her head at me and sighed. We were trading sisterly words about this crazy nigga with just our eyes, and our words weren't too nice. I met Kenny upstairs and shut and locked the door. I fell back on the couch and popped open my Teddy Grahams, glad that Dash was out of my sight.

"That nigga do be whylin'," said Kenny as he kicked off his shoes and took a seat next to me. I turned my body and rested my legs across his lap. Without having to ask him, he took my Nike's off and began to give a foot rub through my socks. I just about fell in love.

I put the television on STARZ since The Crazies was playing, and I'd never got through the entire movie before. Kenny moved the massage up my leg and sooner than later he was massaging between my thighs, two fingers making circles through my stretch denim pants. Probably wouldn't make it to the end this time, either.

"Kenny…" my voice fell faint and my body fell limp. The bag of Teddy Grahams was on the ground. I didn't notice when my eyes closed, but when they opened, Kenny's steel gray eyes were over me, staring into me, stealing my breath away.

With Kenny I didn't have to give instructions or hint at anything. His every move was the right move. His every guess was my next idea. He unzipped my pants and helped me slip them off, then ducked down and simply slid the draws to the side to get some work done. He knew how to use his luscious, lovely lips, oh so well. I grabbed at his back and moaned his name softly, although I'd told myself I wouldn't make a noise. Hearing myself have sex embarrassed me. It sounded so silly. But Kenny's head was no joke. I just bit my tongue, dropped my guard, and let the good feelings roll.

4

Dash didn't just drop me off and leave this time. He came inside.

I hated when he was here. All the little hoes I worked with crowded him like pigeons. The money he threw was the bread, and it burned me up when he came in here trying to flaunt his shit. He had a son, he had me, I had a new son or daughter coming, and there was nothing he loved more than to come in my workplace and throw money away just to look like the nigga with the biggest bank roll. A smart nigga would be stacking chips for a rainy day.

I felt like he was trying me when he did this shit. Especially because he already heard all the stories I stayed telling him about how these trifling bitches in here were jealous that I could claim him. You would think he would come in here and look out, maybe just tip only me. Yeah, right. It made him feel better to have the other bitches begging his pockets and doing tricks for him like lap dogs. They stayed trying to test me, and God forbid one got him to throwing his money. They would stare me down and laugh at me like I was a silly goose. Shit pissed me off to the core. Of all the strip clubs in Atlanta, Strokers *had* to be his club of choice.

I got dressed in the back, lotioned up, put my makeup on, redid my lashes, tightened my shoes, and mentally prepared for another night of the naked hustle and extra degradation. I walked out unnoticed. Most of the crowd was around the main stage while a dancer named Rabbit and her girls hooked it up for her birthday set. I found work in a corner soon enough.

A regular, they called him Bright, was the darkest nigga in his whole crew. He always wore all black. Always threw money in here like he had a black card, too. He usually didn't fuck with me, but only because his business partner Dougie was a fool for me. When Dougie came through he showed me love. Always. Not to complain, but it literally got to the point where other niggas are afraid to tip me if he's here. He'd taken a personal liking to me. But Dougie wasn't here tonight.

Bright pulled me close so I could hear him. "Take care of me and my boys tonight. We got you, baby."

"Where's Dougie?" I asked. I didn't want to upset the nigga if he was in the building and make him jealous by rubbing up on niggas in his own crew. I could not fuck up my money that way. Dougie's money was *good* money.

"He had to take care of some shit tonight. I won't tell." Bright smiled and revealed his jagged teeth. Bright yellow. True to his name. "You want a drink?"

I shook my head. If Dash cared to notice me in here taking a cup to the head, no telling how he would flip on me later. "Ya'll need private rooms or what?"

"You good right here."

I was nervous about dancing with them in front of everyone, including other dancers. Bitches was fucked up like that. They'd be quick to make it seem like I was happily flexing on my main customer by selling it to his right hand man, satisfied if they could fuck up my cash flow. Everyone knew that Dougie liked to think he had me to himself. He let anyone tip me on the stage, but on the floor, he held it down. Dash didn't interfere.

Without any more questions I got to work. I was feeling a little more dizzy than usual, but I shook it off. Thankfully a slower Chris Brown jam was in rotation. I'd be able to keep my moves slow and sultry. I kept swaying and rolling my body on his crew. Soon enough the money began to flow. I was surrounded by at least six dudes. Dollar bills and five and tens fell across my body, landing in a pile at my feet.

One nigga pulled me by the arm and onto his lap. He motioned at my breast and I politely moved his palms away. They were tender as hell these days. Plus, I didn't take too well to niggas touching me, in general. Maybe because they seen me let Dougie do it, they thought it was okay for them to do the same. I let Dougie do it every now and then just as a bonus for his loyalty, but they were learning quickly that they did not share the same privileges. They weren't too happy about that.

The one I was giving the lap dance to leaned forward after I nudged his hands away. He came so close into my face our noses almost touched. I was nervous, wondering what the fuck he was trying to do. "You gotta give me a little somethin', shawdy. Let a nigga touch that soft ass skin you got."

His breath reeked like dark liquor and beer, mixed with garbage juice and sour milk. Added to my pre-existing dizziness, I couldn't take it. I hopped up and ran to the back, and lost my late dinner in a trash can. The girls in the dressing room all paused and watched, and then laughed and made comments to each other, inaudible over my heaving and gagging.

"I be telling these bitches all the time that mixing pills and liq is never no good," laughed one of them while walking past me back onto the floor. Only one dancer was left in the back once I finally lifted my head out of the giant garbage can. She sat in the corner fixing her lipstick.

"You need water, Sunshine?"

"Please, Bubbles. Please. Bottled water if you can get one?"

She closed her makeup bag, nodded, and popped in a fresh stick of gum. "Want one?"

I nodded. She went out to the bar and returned a few minutes later. I was in the mirror retouching my makeup. Throwing up always caused my eyes to water ridiculously. She set it on the counter in front of me and popped her gum. "You was dancing with Dougie's crew over by the DJ, weren't you?"

"Yeah…why?"

"And you left all that money on the floor?"

Fuck. I already knew what the fuck was going on. "Who's dancing over there now?" I asked, snatching up my shit in a hurry.

"Them two young bitches who be back here fucking each other. You know who I'm talking about?"

My head bobbled up and down as I stood, quickly zipping my bags closed.

"Go get yo' shit. Look like when they done they gonna be picking all that shit up. They makin' guap out there on your pile."

"Fuck!" I grabbed the water bottle, rushed out to the floor, and found the same two bitches she mentioned – Brooklyn and Red – out there shaking they ass in my spot. On my money. And them dumb niggas were throwing more up into the air, mixing their profit with mine.

Without a word I pushed through the dudes and crouched down; began scooping up my money.

"She back ya'll," slurred Bright. Obviously drunk.

"Excuse me?" Brooklyn snapped. "What the fuck you doing?"

I looked up at her and said nothing, but I never stopped grabbing up the dollar bills.

"Ay, that's our fucking money!" Red shouted.

I stood up, and dared the both of them with my eyes. "I was dancing over here, first. Now ya'll saw this fucking money on the floor when ya'll came dancing ya'll asses over here and you mean you ain't even give a fuck? You was just gonna claim my shit? I'm picking up my fucking money. That's what the fuck I'm doing."

I got back in a squat to continue scooping the money into my bag, and Brooklyn bent over and tried to snatch the shit away from me. I pushed her by the leg and almost caused her to fall. "Get the fuck back! Make your own fuckin' money, hoe!"

"You grabbing up all the shit he threw on us, too! This shit ain't even right!"

"Not my fucking problem."

"Ay, all three of you can put it down for us, shawdy. No need to fight," one of his boys said, resting his hand on my shoulder. I shook his hand off.

"It don't work like that." I was almost done raking it all up when Red kicked my hand with her sharp ass stilettos.

"You are NOT finna take all our fucking money!"

"Ouch, bitch!" I tightened my bag closed and stood straight up, ready to swing. Red pushed me first and I grabbed onto her before flying all the way back. I started swatting at her face. I wasn't a good fighter, but I did know that if you scratched and slapped and punched enough, something was bound to connect and hurt.

Brooklyn grabbed onto my bag and took my attention away from Red, and I turned to slap her hands away before slapping her in the face. Brooklyn stumbled back into a table and held her face while Red was fighting back and pulling my hair. I took a palm to the face, too, but continued to scratch at her skin. We had each other by the hair when the bouncers came and grabbed us apart. She was still kicking at me, but I was glad they interrupted. It all happened so quickly that I forgot my situation and became more scared than upset. I didn't take any blows to the stomach or back, and I was grateful.

Dash showed up in the mix and eyeballed me crazily. I didn't even realize the whole club had come to a standstill. "What the fuck is wrong with you?!"

I ignored his question and let the bouncer drag me back into the dressing room. I had my bag in one piece and all my money inside, and now that I was calming down, that was all that mattered. I was feeling sick again, actually. I'd taken the water Bubbles was nice enough to bring to me and left the shit out there on the floor.

"Nick, can I get some ice?"

The big bodied, football-framed security guard crossed his arms and stood blocking the dressing room door.

"Not 'til the boss gets back here."

I huffed and sat down, put my feet up on the counter and leaned my head back, eyes closed. "I don't feel good, Nick. I need ice, ice water, or something."

"You got a problem holding your liquor, Sunshine?"

That voice wasn't Nick's voice. I opened my eyes, and focused on Ron, the manager of the club. "Ronnie, I'm the farthest fucking thing from drunk."

"Well there has to be a reason you lost your damn mind and broke out a fight in my spot."

"Bitches was tryna be slick about taking my money. They tried ganging up on me and you can run the cameras on that. I ain't with that shit. Simple as that. I didn't go over there to start no fight. All I was trying to do was pick up my money and they had a problem with that. Ask the niggas that was over there. Dougie's crew. Ask them who was dancing there first. Go 'head."

"I ain't askin' shit. We getting good money in the door tonight, and ain't no one fucking that up. You can get ya shit together and go home. They're gonna have to get the fuck out, too. You know my policy. You ain't coming back till' I get five hundred in cash. Plus your tip out. And your tip in. Tip the DJ and leave."

"Whatever," I sighed. "I don't need to be in here, anyway." I opened my bag, counted out thirty dollars for the DJ, handed it to Nick and he handed it to Ron.

"Get ya shit together."

"I heard you the first fucking time."

He left the dressing room and Nick tried leaving behind him.

"You still gonna bring me some ice, Nick? Please?" He nodded and left. A rush of girls came in once he left the doorway. When there's a fight, no one is allowed in or out of the dressing room until whoever fought is taken to the back and talked to. I wasn't even on no wild shit. I just wanted to go home, anyway. This early ending to my night probably cost me a good thousand, though. All I had in my bag probably didn't pass four-hundred dollars.

Girls were staring at me while they pretended to do makeup. Some were even trying to joke me into telling them what happened. I wasn't giving any of those hoes my attention. Nick came back with a cup of ice water and I gladly accepted. By then I was dressed back in my regular clothes, had my bag packed up and all. Dash was waiting right outside the doorway when I left the dressing room and grabbed my arm aggressively. I was ready to swing, but I caught my breath when I saw his face. "The fuck? You scared the shit out of me!"

"Ay yo, shut the fuck up, man. What the fuck you doing fighting and shit?"

"Look, it happened and it's over with. I'm ready to go. You ready?"

He let go of my arm and gave me the serious face. "You trying the shit out of me, shawd'."

"And them bitches was trying the shit out of me. My money is my money. Fuck that. Let's go."

I felt eyes on me and glanced around the club. Ron was watching me from the bar. I acknowledged him, nodding his way, and began walking for the door. Dash had no choice but to follow. I bet them bitches were mad he had to leave just because I cut his night short and blocked his money, but oh well. They tried hard to use him to make the fool out of me, but like always, they were reminded who really ran this shit.

5

Bop Bop Bop Bop.

"Shit!"

I pushed Kenny off me and slid down from the kitchen counter. We scrambled like headless chickens to pick up and separate our clothes from the living room floor. "What time is it?!" I asked in a frenzy. Kenny glimpsed at his watch as he slid his pants back on.

"Almost two," he replied while hopping to get his second leg in.

I clasped my bra closed and pulled it up over my shoulders. I barely had my panties on when the door knocked again.

"Fuck! It's too early for her to be back. Fuck, fuck. Kenny, you got your pants on so just answer the door for me!" I grabbed the rest of my clothes and fled into Tonnie's room. By the time I was pulling my shirt over my head, Tonnie knocked on the door, and peeked her head through the crack.

"Permission to enter my room?"

I stood still, looking guilty, afraid to make eye contact. When I finally did, she had a budding smile on her face. I couldn't keep a straight face either, and we busted out laughing together. "Caught ya'll in the act, huh?"

"If only ya'll came back in like five more minutes. We weren't in here with it, though…"

"Damn, sorry." Laughing, she set her bag down on the bed and went to the dresser to pull out a change of clothes. "Well, Dash is staying for the night so I could be busy in a little while, myself. I don't care what ya'll doing."

As if he heard his name, he came and poked his head through the doorway, walking in once he saw that I was decent. I would've preferred him to knock, but his sense of respect was all messed up.

"Shawdy gets it in," he laughed, but I wasn't cool with him like that to joke on that level.

Tonnie shook him off and brought my attention back to her. "Well, G, I'm about to hit the shower. My night turned bad. Early. I just wanna lay down. Whatever ya'll get into out there, just keep it down, aight?"

"Cool," I exited the room as soon as possible. Count on Dash to come in and make any moment uncomfortable. I was ready to get away from any space where he was, but Tonnie's last comment made me wonder if she wanted to talk about it. I kinda wanted some alone time with my sister, but both of our guys were here and that was too much to ask at the moment.

When I stepped out of her room, Kenny was chilling on the couch, undershirt on with his outer shirt around his neck. He looked at me a little unsure. I shook my head with a smile. "She ain't trippin."

He took a deep breath and sat back, a little more relaxed. I already knew he was concerned about disrespecting her place. But she wasn't on that. My sister and I were really close. She didn't judge me half as much as I judged her. I guess it had a lot to do with her being the older sister. My parents always put so much heat on her to be the responsible one and treated me like the baby, and I guess due to that, I looked up to her and carried some of their expectations. It wasn't really fair, but it was what it was.

I took my place on the couch with him and laid out across his lap. What we had going on was way too good. I needed that. He almost read my mind.

"You cool down yet?"

"What you mean?" He couldn't see my face but I was smirking my ass off.

"What you mean, what I mean? You know what I'm talking about. Up on the kitchen counter, huh? Freak."

"What? That was your idea!"

He chuckled. "I know. I'm just tryna get you to stop playin' silly. Ginger, you got it."

I laughed and sat up to face him. "What you mean, 'I got it'?"

"You get it wetter than that thang!"

We laughed good and hard. Whenever he put "that thang" on the end of a sentence it sounded ridiculous and he knew I cracked up every time. Using "that thang" in reference to my "thang" just made it even funnier.

"So what she say?"

I shrugged. "It's no biggie. According to her she 'bout to get it in her damn self, so she said she don't care what we do out here. Whatever we do, just keep it down. Those were her exact words."

"Oh really?" He grabbed me up and snuggled up to my neck, placed a soft kiss here, placed his full lips there. I almost got caught up in his scent all over again but I shifted away and took hold of my desires.

"I'd rather just get a blanket and cuddle up. I'm not comfortable anymore…with Dash here." He looked at me like he didn't understand. "Just the chances of him coming out here and…I just really, *really* don't like him. Is that okay?"

An awkward second went by, but he shrugged and agreed. "It's fine. Now I'm mad I was holding back. I shoulda put it all on ya' when I had the chance."

"Cumming doesn't make the sex anything less than awesome, if the sex was awesome. I'll just take a rain check." That made him smile. He wasn't the average guy, but all guys could go for a stroke to the ego every now and then.

I woke up later to some noise in the kitchen. Kenny was still underneath me on the sofa, knocked out. I wiped my eyes out to focus and figure out who it was moving around in there. The figure was small, so it had to be Tonnie. I got up from the couch as carefully as possible not to stir Kenny, and tipped across the living room floor. Tonnie was in there, slamming cups and bowls out of the cabinets, tears running down her face.

"Sis, you okay? What's wrong? The sun is coming up. Shouldn't you be sleeping?" She jumped at the sound of my voice and tried to turn her face away, but I'd already seen that she was crying.

"I'm fine. Just looking for something. I'm hungry."

"What you need? I'll reach it."

"Ginger, just go back to sleep. Please."

"Tonnie? Tonnie. Look at me. What's wrong?"

She faced me with water in her eyes and her face all screwed up. Her nose was red from trying to hold back her feelings. Mine would get red the same way so I knew she was trying to look normal and it just wasn't working.

"Sis, why are you crying? It's got to be like five or six in the morning. Tell me what's wrong. You in pain or something?"

"It's nothing. I'm getting way too emotional over stupid shit. I hate this. Dash, he just pissed me off. That's it. And now I'm hungry and I don't know what I want."

"Oh…he didn't put his hands on you or anything, right?" She refused to give me details until this day, but I wasn't going to forget about that bruise she had several weeks ago.

"No. Hell no. Nothing like that."

I sighed relief. "Oh. Okay. Well you hungry? Why don't he take you to get something?" I asked while yawning.

"Girl, he been left. Ya'll must've been sleep." Tonnie sniffled and wiped her face, and then apologized for waking me.

"Sis, are you serious? We gotta get up soon to get dressed anyway if we plan on getting to school on time. I wanted to have a little alone time with you all day. I don't care. So what about some cereal? You in the mood for that? Cuz I'm about to make some." She shrugged. We poured out two bowls and went into her room. We sat on the bed and she switched the TV on cartoons.

"So how's it going? Still getting sick?"

"Yeah," she nodded while crunching. "Got sick at the club last night. That's what started the problem. Ended with a fight. Can't go back until I pay $500. And Dash won't give me the money." She took another bite. "Shit pissed me off so bad."

"That's what ya'll got into it about? Wait; *you* were fighting?" The last question came out louder than I meant it to.

"Hush, girl. Yeah. These girls were trying to pick up my money and I don't play that shit."

"Tonnie…that was so not smart."

"Fuck 'em."

"I'm not talking about them. I'm talking 'bout you. Not cool."

"Mommy? Mommy is that you? When you got here?"

I shoved her playfully. "Shit, I *wish* Mommy was here. I need some of her turkey wings and greens right now. Damn..." Both of our fat asses sat silent for a moment just reminiscing about our mother's great cooking. But I snapped back to the point.

"So what did he say that made you so mad, exactly?"

"Girl, I don't really want to take it there, but the point is, he'll go in there and throw money in the air for the other girls, but when it comes to me, he act like he don't want to associate with me and shit. And inside the club, that's fine. But outside the club, you my nigga and I'm supposed to come first. I asked him to give me the money to pay my fine for fighting, and he told me no. All cuz he don't want me to go back to work there anymore."

For the first time in life, I couldn't believe I was thinking it, but I agreed with Dash. "Sis, I don't really like you working there, either. I'll just be real. You're pregnant. The two just don't mix."

"Ginger. This nigga has the money for it, though. Why would you spend it all on the next bitch but your baby momma that you're in a relationship with can't get five hundred dollars so that I can pay my bills?"

"Tonnie. In some strange way, despite how he treats you, some part of him must care for you enough to not want to see you in there pregnant. I'm sure you're not gonna be in there trying to dance full term, but even now when you're not showing. All that smoke in the air and loud music around you, it's not good for a developing baby."

She sighed like she was defeated. "Ginger, I need to make money. Somehow. This shit is ridiculous. I know he has the ends to pay my bills for me, but I hate depending on him. I can't take that."

It looked like she was getting to that point, and I didn't want to push her there all over again. If anything, I was glad I had her calm. So I left it alone. Maybe I could help her get a regular job.

6

Man, I didn't have patience for Tonnie's whining and bitching. Hell nah I wasn't about to give her money just to go back to that shit. She wasn't tryna listen to a nigga when I said I didn't want my baby around all that smoke and all them drunk niggas. So what does she do? She turns around and gets in a fucking fight. Kicking and swinging, just being fucking stupid. Anything could have happened. I was really heated after that. And then she think she just gonna fuck a nigga, then ask for the money like pussy makes me forget she fucked up.

Yeah, right. Wrong nigga. She pissed me the fuck off with that dumb shit. So I got up and left.

I was right in front of my place when I got a call. Someone way back off 285 N was tryna get some work. I was sleepy as fuck and I didn't want to turn around and go handle that, but it was a quick come up. I fought myself awake all the way to the Chamblee Tucker exit and met with my dude Jacob in a Walgreens plaza. We parked aside each other in the far end of the lot, away from passing cars and cameras. Jacob turned his car off when he saw me, came over, and got into the passenger side.

"You ain't know you needed more work until six in the morning, dude? I was finally at my spot about to lay it down, man. What you need?"

"How much you got on you? I'm runnin' low. I got about seven hundred on me. How much you gonna give me for that?"

I could have stuck this fool up. You never put out your chips first to make a trade. For all he knew I could just pull out the heat and leave him broke and out of stock, all at the same time. Jacob was good business, though. A little amateur, but solid. Flipped what he needed to flip. Plus, I was way too tired to go through with all that at the moment. Tonnie had a lot of shit on a nigga mind. So I guess for now, an even trade would do.

"I got a half brick. Take it or leave it. It's good shit. You can flip it twice if you do it right."

Usually, simple transactions like these took half as much time and never included advice, but Jacob was a young nigga, probably like 19 years old, tryna hustle and establish his own. I admired the kid, but he was still a bit lost on how some of this shit worked. I could tell by the way he went about shit. That's another reason I decided to just make a clean deal. We all started out somewhere.

He seemed excited. "Where it's at?"

I reached in the backseat and felt like he was watching my movements too closely. "Keep ya eyes forward, my dude."

He spun his head back around on request and kept his eyes down in his lap. I reached back again and pulled up the back seat to pull out the saran wrapped package of hard. I put the seat back the way it was, and looked out all the windows to make sure no one was watching from far away. Anyone could be trying to set you up at any given time. That just came along with the profession.

We switched interests and once that was taken care of, I was right back on the highway on the way to the crib.

I tucked away my stash safely, glad that I took the time to go up my funds real quick. Tonnie didn't know it, but she had me feeling like stepping up and taking care of her for the long run. I wanted to do the same for Shakima back in the day, but it was her attitude that fucked that up. Always talking down to a nigga. Always tryna tell a nigga I ain't shit. She could keep that shit. I wasn't for it. So I kept it moving. And all of a sudden I became the bad guy. I hustle, yeah. I do what I need to do, but she could never say that I didn't provide for my boy.

Tonnie on the other hand, she was snappy, had a mouth on her, but I would be lying if I said I didn't like that shit. I wasn't the type of nigga to outright let a bitch know that I was in love, but I was really hoping Tonnie would start taking this situation seriously and just let me take care of her. I had the money. I was stacking more than she thought. The money I threw in the club and the way it pissed her off – I didn't expect her to understand – but that was only pocket change. I had almost seventy-five grand saved up. With the new circumstances, I needed her to understand that she'd be set once she dropped our kid. And I didn't want her working in that damn club anymore. I was ready to lock it down with her. She just didn't trust me. That being said, wasn't no way for me to properly tell her without it leading to an argument.

There was a lot a nigga wanted to tell her, but I just felt like admitting certain things would be against my code and would make me look too soft. I wanted to tell her that I wanted a baby girl that looked just like her. I wanted to tell her that after she carried this thing out, we could move back to where my momma lived in Moultrie and she could relax in that big ass house while I got something legit running. We could lay low there until we had enough to get our own place, with two extra rooms for my baby girl and my son. I wasn't that different from the next man. I wanted to have a family that I could support, too. Most of all I wanted Tonnie and my kids to be set. Tonnie deserved a lot more than me, but since I had her, I wanted to make that shit happen for her. But she was so fucking stubborn. She didn't want to let me.

7

I kept missing Kaycee before she got to work, so I walked over to her shop while she was there and just paid the money to have my hair done. A good touch up was only going to cost about seventy dollars, anyway. I didn't have that much leave-out to re-press. My homegirl deserved it the way she kept my hair hooked up at all times. I didn't mind.

I liked the shop she worked at a lot. It was classy. Always neat. A well run black-owned business. I was waiting for her chair to open up, flipping through the VIBE magazine I found on the coffee table, and listening to the topic of conversation going around the shop. All the women were putting their two cents in on how they felt about the strip clubs in Atlanta: which one was the best one, which one had the prettiest girls, what kind of bodies they wish they had, and at the moment, the heated discussion was how they felt about their men going there.

Kaycee and I slipped each other knowing eyes every now and then. She knew why I was making some of the facial expressions I was making, and every time someone would say some ignorant shit about stripping, talk about how nasty strippers were, or say something offensive in general, I would look up from the magazine, make a face, then look to Kaycee, and she'd already be giggling to herself.

I didn't add to the discussion because I'd hurt too many feelings. Some of these women thought that being a dancer made you some crazy, freak nasty type of person and they didn't understand that a job was a job. One or two women in the place were motivated by strippers and felt like it was the life to have. They were hooked on the glamorous side, and it wasn't all about that, either. I wasn't a counselor and I wasn't worried about changing anyone's mind. At most, the discussion taking place was entertaining as hell.

I checked my phone every now and then, waiting for Dash to

text message me back. I was waiting for him to bring me a six-piece hot teriyaki and fries from Xpress Wings around the block, and like usual, he was running super late.

Kaycee finally called me up to the chair and sat me down. "Girl, how the hell did we get all on this subject? Ain't they crazy?" She whispered.

I nodded. "It damn sure got a little offensive in here for a second. I'm not even tripping. People talk a lot when it comes to shit they know nothing about."

"I heard that." She spun me around and pumped me up in the salon seat. "What I'm supposed to be doing now?"

"Re-press my leave out and the layers between the tips. They're frizzy and shrinking. And I might need my ends trimmed. You tell me."

Kaycee got to work and conversation died down around the entire shop for a while. Feeling her small fingers working in my hair was beginning to put me to sleep. I would've been able to doze off if it weren't for my raging stomach. She had parted my hair and clipped it up into sections, and was combing out the hair to press and restyle it by the time Dash came through the door.

He had my food in hand, a peach tea in his other, and a smile on his face like he'd finally got it right this time. I took a deep breath and closed my eyes. Told myself not to nag just this once. He was always late no matter what, but at least he came, and now I could eat.

"My muthafuckin' nigga Dash." Kaycee broke the silence in the place with her excited ass greeting, and Dash nodded to her while handing the Styrofoam box to me. The food felt a little cold, but I swallowed down the urge to lash at him and thanked him politely for bringing it. Dash smiled. I forgave him instantly.

These hormones had me swinging back and forth. Sometimes I hated him and I could argue all night, and other times I was in love with him like I'd never loved before. And at this moment, with his smile, just like that he had me head over heels.

Kaycee broke my trance and asked, "You ever thought about putting some color in this? I think if you put a little honey in the front of this, with your complexion? It would really pop, girl. Trust me."

"Uh…yeah. But how much does coloring cost here?"

"No, girl. We can do it later tonight."

I was about to object and tell her I had to work, but then I remembered. No work for me. "Alright."

Dash rubbed my arm and nudged the box in my lap. "The food okay?"

I nodded. "Yeah. Thanks again, babe. What you about to do?"

"About to pick up my son and take him to play…or some shit. Just get at me lata, aight?"

I nodded obediently and watched Dash leave. I wished there were more days where we just spent time together. I was going to get that nigga to slow down and pay attention to me and only me one of these days. When it was about his money or his son, I tried not to be a big baby and get in the way, but damn he was leaving me needy. Other than sex, we didn't share too many good times together.

Kaycee cut into my thoughts once again. "So what you gonna do now that you can't go back to the club?"

"I can," I finished swallowing a bite of chicken. "Just when I pay the money."

"Keep your head still," she commanded. "Uh…well what you going to do until then? If you need a job just let me know. You know I got you."

"A job working where? Doing what?"

"Oh there you go. Why you gotta answer like that? Yeah, chick. An actual real life job."

"And mine isn't a real life job because what?"

"You know damn well what I mean. You the one that made it seem like I was speaking blasphemy. There's more than one way to get paid. That's all I'm saying."

"Whatever, Kaycee. I'm not sure about anything I'm about to do so if I think that should be my next step I'll let you know."

"If you say so, Tonnie. You can't dance all your life," she mumbled.

I rolled my eyes. Kaycee was borderline preachy sometimes and I just wasn't in the mood for it. Dash came in and put me on a cloud, and she was knocking me down. Spoiling my mood. I dropped it. Nothing more on that subject.

Only twenty minutes more passed and she was finished with me. I don't know why I expected it to take longer. I took my phone out to call Dash and maybe ask if I could come along and play with his son, but my phone was dead. I was halfway out the door after paying Kaycee, but I spun around and rushed back in.

"Kaycee, real quick. Let me see your phone, please? Mine went dead."

I knew Dash's number by heart. I was worried the most about him not picking up to an unknown number, so I texted him instead. All I said was that I'd be home if he wanted to bring his son over, and I wouldn't mind tagging along if they went out to do something. Either way, he knew where to find me until I charged my phone. I thanked Kaycee again for this fire ass hair style, and then I left.

I walked inside Burger King on the way home and sat down to enjoy a spicy chicken sandwich meal, but the thought of missing Dash's call or him showing up without me being home yet caused me to rush through it. By the time I walked through my door, I felt heartburn budding in my chest. I took some Pepto and sat my ass down, hooked my phone up to the wall, and waited. I fell asleep waiting, actually.

I didn't wake up until Kaycee called after she got off work. It had to be after nine if that was the case. I told her she could come over and we could do the color tonight just to get it out the way. Once that was established we hung up and I checked through my phone and all my messages.

Dash hadn't called once. That was rude. I wondered why he always kept me from his little boy. Truth was, I just wanted to get some practice in.

8

She was in a funky mood when she let me in her place, but what the hell was new? Her and Kaycee were set up in the kitchen, doing some shit to her hair. I sat down on her couch and found the remote. Sat there wondering how long this hair thing was going to take. She just got her shit done earlier so I was confused as hell. I was glad that was a female type of thing.

"You ate?" I asked.

She played like she didn't hear me, but there was a big ass opening in the wall through to the kitchen, so I knew my voice could easily be heard. I left it alone and put my attention back to the television. When I looked back in that direction, Tonnie and Kaycee were talking, but Kaycee was staring at me. I looked away and tried not to stunt her, but the pictures she sent to my phone earlier were hard to forget. One side of me wanted to put the bitch on blast. I mean, she was grimy as hell for that, but the nigga in me said to let it ride for a second. As long as I looked and didn't touch, there wasn't any trouble in it for me. But shit never ever worked like that.

I just sat there. I didn't say anything. Kaycee felt like she was a badder bitch than Tonnie, and she was tryna show me. I didn't know what her point was or where the hell this was coming from. Tonnie was going to remain in the picture for a long time due to our situation, so I had no clue what Kaycee had up her sleeve. This shit was all new to me. I was still lost as hell.

But Kaycee wasn't. Between focusing on Tonnie's hair and me, it seemed like she knew exactly what she was doing. When Tonnie wasn't looking, I locked eyes with Kaycee and made a face like *What?* She broke a smile and shook her head. I shrugged it off. Shawdy was definitely up to something.

I got lost in my own little world after that. I separated myself from those two in there doing their girl thing. I didn't want to tempt the situation by giving Kaycee any more attention. Truthfully, I felt bad that I even came over. I wasn't planning on it.

I got Tonnie's message earlier about wanting to come out with me and my son, but picking up my son was already a lie I told just to get out of her grip with no questions asked. I wasn't with my boy. I was out pushing weight. I chilled in the studio half the time I was out, but I hated to tell her about that because she always made it seem like I chose the studio over her. She felt the studio was just an excuse to use when I didn't feel like doing shit. Partially true, but I did get shit done at the studio more than she thought.

I was planning to call it a night after that until Kaycee texted me out of nowhere. At first I thought Tonnie was still with her, but after she said what's up and asked what I was up to, she followed that message with some picture messages and let me know how she really felt. I was going to delete the messages and just go home, but she told me to come find her at Tonnie's. That she'd be waiting to see me then.

And here I was.

I felt bad as shit for this. Tonnie was none the wiser. I wasn't no soft nigga, but I still had a conscience. Tonnie told me that Kaycee been her ace since the tenth grade. What could make a bitch stab her best girl in the back like that? A chance at some dick? The more I thought about it and stole glances at Kaycee, the more I became disgusted with her. I would have to dead this shit quick. The way she kept looking at me, shit was sure to spin out of control.

Kaycee excused herself from the kitchen and went into Tonnie's room to the bathroom. Tonnie shot me a cold grimace and turned away.

"What's ya problem?"

"Dash, please. I'm not in the mood."

"Not in the mood for what? I didn't even say anything. Why you actin' that way?"

"Why didn't you call me? You knew I wanted to hang out. You never let me see Quani. I feel some type of way about that."

I didn't want to deal with her attitude any longer so I decided to just spill the truth. Or at least a partial truth. "Tonnie, look. I went to go pick up Quantrell but Shakima started tripping again. We got into an argument and after that I dipped and went to the studio to clear my head for a few. I was upset today. It wasn't nothing against you. You see I'm here now, right?"

She rolled her eyes but I knew she wasn't going to stay mad now that I gave a reasonable explanation. Kaycee returned from the bedroom and shot a sly look on her way to Tonnie. They immediately started going back and forth in female cackles, so I zoned out and tuned back into ESPN.

Right then, my phone buzzed in my lap. New picture message. Same number all the others came from. This chick was slick. The picture took a second to load when I opened the message. What showed up was a picture of Kaycee in Tonnie's bathroom. A booty shot. The picture showed her from the waist down, posing her ass for the camera phone, an ass that would have been completely naked if not for the tiny thong she had on. The caption said, "Like my lace?", plus a peach emoji.

Although the picture was sexy as hell, Kaycee was coming off way too greasy for my liking. She actually seemed a little desperate. It was too many niggas out there for her to be tryna shove herself down my throat. She was bold for trying to do it this way, but shit was getting too hot in here. I felt uncomfortable, and that wasn't normal for me. I had to get up out of there.

I stood and stretched, tossed my phone in my pocket, and picked up my keys. I went into the kitchen and kissed Tonnie goodbye. I didn't even acknowledge Kaycee when I turned my back to them and headed for the door.

9

"Damn, Tonnie. Picked up on the first ring? Expecting a call?" I joked.

"Nah," she sounded tired like she had been sleeping. But it was one in the afternoon. She slept like a bat. "I saw it was you and picked up in a hurry. I thought something was wrong. You never call. Everything okay?"

"Everything is cool, Sis. I was calling with some news."

"What's up?"

"I made a few calls. I understand that you don't want to have to lean on that fucking creep hand on foot soooo…I found a job for you."

She was silent for a while. But I heard her breathing. "Ginger. A job where?"

"You have good people skills right? And I know your looks and personality can take you far, so I think this is a perfect start, even if it's only temporary. Plus, you can pull tip money just like your old job."

"You still haven't told me where."

"On top of that, they're desperate to hire new people because they had a bad review and half the staff had to go. This would be too easy to pass up. I almost took the damn job my damn self. Shit, if it weren't for evening classes…"

"Ginger. The place. Please."

"Chili's."

"Chi-girl, what? I'm supposed to be a waitress? In who's world?"

I let out an aggravated breath. "Tonnie. So tell me what you'd like to be doing? Since you can't dance at the moment and you know you won't be dancing in a few months, tell me what kind of job you'd settle for, then. I'm just trying to help you out. Anything so I don't have to watch that dummy put a leash on you."

"First of all, I'm not a dog so I'll never have a leash. Dash and I don't have a typical relationship but the nigga does look out for me. Maybe on his own time, but he does what he needs to do for me. Don't get that twisted. Second of all Sis, I'm glad you have my back, but I told you already. When I figure out what I want to do I'll let you know. I'm not tryna bust my ass at no restaurant just to get paid three dollars an hour. My home girl Vivica used to do that shit at Outback and she was always broke. I'm so straight off that. Thanks, but no thanks."

"So, you're not even going to think about it. I'm telling you, Tonnie. You'd have this job by next week. Stop short changing yourself. You don't know what kind of success you could make of it. I'm sure Vivica wasn't getting tipped stupidly because she wasn't that good of a waitress. You know how to work people. You know you do. Why do you automatically cut yourself out of opportunities? You cannot live your whole life thinking it doesn't get better than shaking your ass on a Friday night."

"What did you say?"

"Tonnie." I took a deep breath just to calm myself, but she was pissing me off. She was my sister and we got into it plenty of times, but I had to remind myself that because she was my sister, I had to have patience. "I'm sorry. That came out wrong. But I just want the best for you."

"Ginger. I'm over this conversation. Like I said. Thanks, but no thanks."

She hung up, so I put the phone down. I took a long gaze out of my bedroom window and let it go slowly. Tonnie had always been the type you couldn't help if she didn't want to help herself. Stubborn like a mule for as long as I could remember. Frickin' Taurus.

I was in a bad mood after that phone call. I was the younger one, but that didn't mean I didn't feel a sense of responsibility for my sister. It took a while to get her off my mind. Until Kenny called and invited me out to the movies. That cheered me up a whole lot. But that wouldn't be until nine o' clock tonight.

Thank God for my roommate. She came and knocked on the door and we talked for a while. I told her about the movies with me and Kenny, and she kind of volunteered to come with her boyfriend, too. She was cool as hell so I didn't mind. We got hungry somewhere in the conversation, so she offered to take me for something to eat. Asia had a car, so I was more than happy to tag along, especially since she mentioned her plans to head to the mall. That would be the perfect opportunity to cop an outfit for the concert.

I had in mind what sneakers I wanted to wear. A fresh pair of Jordans I'd never worn before because I had nothing in my closet to match. Finding an outfit to go along wasn't difficult. By the time we were all done, it was only seven. I was blown. But still excited.

We kicked it in the food court for a while, waiting for Asia's boyfriend to meet us there. And that's where my stomach turned inside out.

I sat extra still hoping Dash wouldn't see me, but if he did, he would have seen the nastiest scowl on my face. He walked into ALDO behind a thick-set chick, shorter and lighter than my sister, but definitely no competition when it came to her physique and her style. I was completely repulsed. I studied their interaction while they were in the store, telling myself not to trip too hard. Chick could've been a cousin or a sister of his, but the kind of person Dash was, that was probably not the case.

Asia pocketed her phone and nudged me in the shoulder. "Ready to go? Brian said to just come meet him on the Macy's side. Foot Locker is over there."

I didn't answer, just stared with the same grimace ingrained in my face. "Ginger. Why you looking so sour? What you looking at?"

I snapped out of it and looked at Asia with a mechanical smile. "Nothing, girl. I'm just thinking of something that wasn't so pleasant. Yeah, I'm ready. Lemme grab my bags." I leaned down under the table right when Dash turned to my direction, and by the time I was done pretending to tie my shoe and grabbed my bags to stand up, he was turned back around facing the other way. The girl he was with looked real grown in the face now that I could get a closer look, and their facial expressions in regards to each other were neutral. No affectionate touches or googly eyes. I peeped all of that in a matter of seconds and felt better after concluding that they had no physical ties. I wasn't going to easily forget her face, though. Just for future reference.

10

Shakima was driving me insane. I was kicking myself for agreeing to this bullshit. She had me out here at the mall on a small shopping spree. That was the terms if I didn't want to pay child support. Every month or so, in addition to getting her whatever she asked for our son, she wanted to go shopping, on me. If throwing half a stack on her every month kept a nigga out of court, I wasn't happy to oblige, but of course I did.

So she had me all up and through Perimeter Mall bored as hell, waiting for her to release me from this slow death sentence. A nigga ain't care about stilettos and purses and fragrances and shit, unless Tonnie was wearing it. She was all that was on my mind. Especially after Kaycee tried to pull that stunt last night. I still had the pictures in my phone. I didn't know what to do with them yet.

These few hours I had to deal with her would have been much more bearable if she brought Quantrell along, but she left him with her sister. She wasn't slick. She knew she kept him away from me at times we could all spend together as a little pretend family. And then the second she would get angry, she was good at making it seem like I was the only reason my son and I didn't spend enough time.

It was getting too late after a while and I had already spent more on her than I planned. I coulda been somewhere taking Tonnie out, which was something I needed to get better with. Sometimes, looking at all the bullshit I put her through, I was surprised she ain't left my ass yet. I just had to get better at expressing certain things.

"Ay, you ready?" Kima was studying another pair of shoes with that look in her eyes. She tried to act like she didn't hear me. "Kima. It's time to go."

She kissed her teeth and rolled her eyes. But she put the damn shoes down. She was going to have to get Roger to buy her those. We were done here.

"You got somewhere to go in a hurry? The mall ain't closing. What's the rush? Your stripper bitch called?"

"Calm that shit down, Kima."

"We only been here not even two hours. What's so important that we can't stay another thirty minutes?"

"Kima. It's time to go. Don't argue. You got enough shit today. Quantrell even has some shit, so you can go home happy. I'm not buying the whole fucking mall for you, and just so you know, yeah. I do wanna see my girl."

That killed her. I saw it all in her face. I would love to know what she'd look like the day she finds out that I have another baby on the way. She didn't know yet, and I didn't know how to tell her. But I felt like I owed Quantrell a report more than I did Shakima. We weren't together, so in my opinion, it wasn't her business. She'd find out eventually.

We left and I was grateful to hit her community and pull up in front her place. I couldn't stand to look at her any longer. I hated that she had the power to grab a nigga by the balls like this. I put the car in park and unlocked the doors. Her twin sister Shameka's car wasn't in the driveway or nothing, but I asked, anyway.

I turned my music down to ask a question. "Quani back yet?"

Shakima didn't look my way, but she stared through the windshield like she was thinking back to something. "What so different about this one? What's she got over me that keeps you from coming and doing the right thing for this family?"

Ah, shit. Not this shit, again.

"Kima, what you talkin' bout? This ain't a family. I care about my son but you know ain't nothing between us. Did Shameka bring him back yet?"

She turned her head to the side like her thoughts were getting deeper. "I remember. All the ways to make you tick. I know how to do it right. You think I forgot?" She shook her head, still staring out ahead. "Nah, I know all the things you like and exactly how you like it. I remember I could make you cum in ten seconds flat…you remember when that happened? Right before I got pregnant with Quantrell. Yup."

By now I was looking at her like she was crazy. I wanted to be as far away from her as possible. She turned and considered me, and took her seatbelt off. Scooted closer. I thought she was just going to get her bags from out the backseat or something, but she surprised me when she put a palm in my lap. She rubbed it in a circle and felt down for my dick through my pants. She wasn't going to find it like that, because it damn sure wasn't hard.

"Shakima, what you tryna do? Back up."

She smirked like she had a plan and unzipped my pants. She didn't stop looking me in the eyes one time. She reached in, pulled out my dick, and started to lean down. I grabbed a fistful of her hair and yanked her head back right before her lips parted on it.

"Get your fucking bags, Kima. Then get the fuck out my car." I flicked her hair loose and her head jerked back. She hit me with an ugly frown, but turned for the car door before the tears in her eyes could drop. She barely got to close the back door before I had the music blasting and was hitting the block at 45 mph.

She had a nigga heart pounding. I don't think I hated another female like I hated Shakima.

11

I was having a terrible day.

Morning sickness had lasted way longer than just the morning. I was hungry as hell because all I did all day was vomit, but everything in my house was shit that I couldn't stand to think about eating. I felt weak, and if my physical condition couldn't get worse, I had a splitting migraine. I took medicine for it but I was sure it came back up during one of the times I had to run for the bathroom.

In addition to all of that, I had a doctor's appointment I really needed but ended up having to reschedule because Dash came to get me twenty minutes too late. Dash was still with me, but I was too irritated to deal with him. He offered to bring me whatever I wanted to eat, but I couldn't concentrate on what was available out there. I had no idea. I just wanted my stomach to stop flipping and my head to stop pounding.

I sat up quickly because I felt warmth rising in my chest, but I moved too fast for my pulsing brain. The pain alone made me gag. Dash jumped up off the edge of the bed and looked at me, helpless. He had no idea what he was supposed to do.

"Out the way!" was the only thing I could say before damn near trampling him to get to the toilet.

"Tonnie, take a hot shower or somethin', shawd'. I can call my mother and ask her what will work…"

I didn't expect him to come up with something like that, and if I wasn't feeling so fucked up I would've thought that was cute. I couldn't hear him after that over the sound of my insides breaking water. I took slow deep breaths and sat upright, leaned against the wall. "Dash. Dash, I need something. I don't have anything left to throw up. Maybe…maybe if I eat my head won't hurt so bad." I wiped tears out of my eyes while Dash started the shower for me.

I wondered why everyone else's pregnancies were so cute. Mine was giving me hell. Times like this, I must admit. I didn't want this shit.

He helped me undress and said, "Look. I don't want you eating fast food today. I don't know much, but that can't be good for you. I'll order from Longhorn or something, to go. Real food. So what do you want? In the mood for anything?"

That was actually a good idea. I stepped into the warm stream and leaned up on the tile. "I don't want chicken. Anything but chicken. No steak. Maybe shrimp. And salad. Potatoes if you can. No pasta. That's too heavy."

"You're not supposed to eat seafood. Didn't you tell me that?"

He needed to just take my order and go. Wasting my voice repeating myself only intensified my headache. "Can't eat it raw. Please, Dash. Try and hurry. Don't take too long."

Surprisingly, he didn't take longer than thirty minutes to come back with my food, which meant one of two things. He either was speeding because to get over to Longhorn's he had to get on the freeway, or their service was faster than McDonalds on a slow day. I'm pretty sure the last option wasn't the case. I figured he was trying to make up for me missing my appointment.

I was covered up in the bed when he returned, and I ate quietly. He didn't go turn on the television, or make a whole bunch of calls on his phone. His phone wasn't even in sight. He just sat at the end of the bed, rubbing my feet through the blankets, and looking at me. That was weird. Wasn't used to that.

Once I finished, I lay down and sighed. Instant relief.

"That help? How was it? You want a cup of ice?"

"No, thank you. That was great. Now I'm just tired. But the motion sickness and the headache. Gone completely. That was easy."

"My lil' girl was tryna tell you something." I looked at Dash with wide eyes. These cutesy little statements were freaking me out. Completely out of his character.

"Dash, you okay?" I had to check to be sure.

"Yeah. I'm good, why?"

"Uh…nothing. How you know it's going to be a girl?"

He shrugged and climbed up on the bed to spread out next to me on top of the sheets. "I don't know, shawdy. I just want it to be. Quani needs a little sister to protect. That will teach him some respect for a woman."

I could hear my sister's laughter coming in from across the city. I refocused and tried to stay in the moment as it was. He was being very serious, so I kept an open mind and responded to this new side of him that I wasn't accustomed to at all. "That's what his mom is for, isn't it?"

"Shit. I don't want to think 'bout that bitch right now."

"That bitch? She's the mother of your child. Weren't you just talking about respecting women? I guess Quantrell does need a little sister cuz I doubt he'll learn about it from you."

One look at Dash, and I could tell I hit a soft spot. Well, at least one of those soft spots he pretends don't exist. "Watch yo' mouth," was all he said. Even though his tone was firm, he wasn't looking my way anymore. I was surprised I'd genuinely made him feel bad.

"Sorry, Dash. I don't know a thing about the relationship between you and Shakima. Sorry I said that. You do okay for me. I shouldn't have said you don't have respect."

He nodded. "Tonnie, real talk. I try. I'm not father-material and a nigga knows that, you feel me? I understand there's probably a smarter, more proper, and more stable nigga out there to give you anything and to be a perfect father and shit. I don't know how to put it in the right words, but all a nigga got is money and a hustle. I'm tryna make it so you can have anything I have. Even if it's not much. You just got to let me show it to you, feel me?"

I couldn't believe I was talking to the same Dash I dealt with every day, but that "in-love" button I'd mentioned? He pressed it and I laid there gawking at him with the big eyes, wishing he'd never leave my life. I wasn't perfect, either, so maybe two not-so-perfect people like us could get together and make it work for the best thing that was about to happen to our relationship.

Dash and I drifted asleep with each other, and it felt like I was living in an unreal world. I wasn't used to him just kicking it with me just because. Two hours later I woke up to my phone ringing. Kaycee was calling.

Kaycee had just called earlier in the morning before Dash showed up, so she said she was just checking up on me. I told her I was good, just laying around with my man, but she insisted she come make sure I was okay. She had two kids already, and said she knew remedies for days like this.

I felt a lot better since earlier, plus I was enjoying one-on-one time with my boyfriend. I politely declined. Kaycee seemed genuinely concerned. I felt kind of bad about brushing her off to the side, but if she had a man she felt this way about she would definitely understand. I didn't sweat it. I cuddled back up to him, and drifted back into my nap.

12

Kenny picked me up from my apartment complex in his cousin's car. He had some cousin who went to Atlanta Tech who'd let him hold his whip every now and then. The original plan was to go to Best Buy to put my laptop in the shop since the damn thing caught a virus, but once that was done, Kenny wasn't finished with me.

He took me to eat at Atlantic Station, and when I complained about my hair needing to be re-done for the concert that weekend, we left and he took me straight to the hair store and then the salon. He was in a good mood I guess, because immediately afterward he took me to get my nails and feet done, too. I stopped him when he suggested we make a curbside order from P.F. Chang's and take our late dinner back to the crib. I had one serious ass question, because Kenny…he didn't have a job.

I caught Kenny's hand on the way out of the nail salon. One step into the parking lot and it was clear that the sun had just gone under for the night. I watched the clouds for a second, trying to figure out how to ask him what I wanted to ask him.

"Uh, Kenny? I have a question. Listen, I appreciate everything after today. *Everything*. You hooked me up. I'm poppin', for real. You're the best for all of this. But um….all of this, plus fifth row tickets…do you have a job I don't know about or something?"

Kenny tensed up and hit the key remote to unlock the car doors. He ran his tongue over his teeth and looked everywhere else so he wouldn't have to look at me. His whole reaction rubbed me the wrong way.

"Kenny? What's the deal? What's going on? You can tell me. I'm just extremely curious."

"I'd rather not speak details," he finally said once we were inside the car.

"Okay, so speak in general terms. How you so hood rich all of a sudden? Net check refunds were over a month ago. I know you not some male stripper somewhere." I laughed at my attempt to lighten the conversation and loosen him up, but I ended up laughing alone. He started the engine. "C'mon, baby. Just be real with me. It's not like I'll say something to someone."

"You ask a lot of questions, babe. You think about things way too hard. Do you need to know where this is all coming from? Or can you just be happy that I'm able to spoil you like you should be spoiled?" He asked that last question with a thumb down my face. That broke me down and momentarily, I was done debating. He seen that his charm worked for a second and reversed out the lot. I wasn't ready to let it go so easily, though.

By the time we were on the 285 I was back to it, again.

"Akendu Olewo."

"You said it wrong."

"Whatever. I'm serious. I'm pushing it not because the answer means so much, but because you're hiding something from me. I'm begging you, tell me, please?"

He rolled the windows down like the air beating through the car would drown out my voice. So I shouted. "Kenny!"

"Mmm…maybe that's what we need to be on next."

"Kenny, don't play." I rolled my window back up and hit him with a serious pouty lip. He looked at me, looked out the window, looked at me, put his eyes on the road, and then sighed. I smirked lightly. Seemed like I was about to win this war.

"Yeah, it's dirty money. You happy? That's your general explanation of what's going on. Any other questions?"

"See? Was that so hard? Dirty money doing what?"

"Ginger, you said general."

"I know. I don't need to know any specifics. I was just offended that you couldn't be open with me. We're better than that."

"Yeah, we are, but that had nothing to do with it. I just don't want you to judge me. You can't stand your sister's boyfriend and you know what kind of business he does. I see how much you hate him and I just like being on your good side. Innocent Kenny."

I sat forward and looked at him crazily. "Boy, you trippin'. You are nothing like Dash, even if *you* were the one that served him *his* work, I would *never* look at the two of you the same. I don't hate him for the work he does. I do think he needs to do something serious with his life if he's going to support my sister and the baby, but the reason I can't stand him is deeper than that. It's the kind of person he is. That's the part that irks me. The way he treats her so bad. I would never judge you. I mean, shit. Get it how you live. At least you're in college and you're working toward something. That's speaks volumes."

He was looking at me between watching traffic like he couldn't believe the words coming from my mouth. "You serious?"

"Yeah. I don't have a personal vendetta against hustlers. Is that what you thought?"

"Something like that, yeah."

"Everyone has a hustle, as far as I'm concerned."

"Yeah? What's your hustle?"

I chuckled. When I said that, I meant everyone except myself.

Kenny was still a knight in shining armor to me no matter what, and he was crazy if he thought I was going to throw him to the waste side just because he got his hands a little dirty. He was an awesome catch.

13

Light bill. Water bill. Gas bill. Rent. Renter's Insurance. Car insurance. Verizon. Within the next two weeks all of that would need to be taken care of, and my savings was going to take a beating since I wasn't doing shit to put that money back in its place. I almost had enough to drive my car from the shop any day now, but no income was pushing any day farther away.

I didn't voice my concerns to Dash. All I did was hint at that five hundred I needed to get back on the pole, and the nigga hung up on me. I hadn't heard from him since. I was sitting in the nail salon with my feet dipped in the pedicure spa, just thinking about money. I needed it like the air I breathed. I hated to feel like I was suffocating. Ginger's offer crossed my mind and stayed lingering like it didn't want to be ignored. I felt like I was backed up against the wall. By the time the tiny Asian lady was painting my toes, I was texting Ginger back and forth about that waitress position. She was more than happy that I'd gotten back to her about it and she claimed she'd be calling them as soon as possible to see what time would be a good time for me to go put in an application.

I was nervous about that whole thing. A little reluctant, even. Staying on my feet wouldn't be a problem – not while I was used to walking around for five to six hours straight on seven inch heels – but handing out food and dealing with complaints, attitudes, indecisiveness…this would all be new to me. I figured I would try it out for a week or two just to see what kind of money I could pull in.

Ginger texted me back in no time and told me we could go up there tomorrow because the manager would give me an interview on the spot. I should've been excited, but I wasn't. Suddenly, I was anxious and all types of agitated. I was motivated to call Ginger and tell her to forget it and then turn to Dash for the funds. My disgust for his jacked up concept of being on-time was enough to keep me from making that call.

Afterward, I went to the Chinese spot across the street from the nail salon and ordered a five piece chicken wing with a side of fries. While I sat there waiting, an all-black Tahoe pulled up with Blueface blasting through the outer-speakers. The Chinese place shook with bass until the car cut off. I rolled my eyes at all these supposed dope boys and ballers riding around putting mortgage payments into their trucks and cars knowing damn well they had all these babies living up in the hood. The cycle of a dumb hustler was just that…dumb. I was comforted by the fact that Dash wanted to be there for our baby. His car was tricked up just a little, but nothing overboard.

A familiar face came inside and locked my gaze.

"Sunshine? Ay, girl. What you doin' over here?"

"I live around the corner."

"Shit…a nigga ain't seen you up in the club a few nights in a row. I heard you got in a fight and shit while I was away. That shit wouldn't have went down like that if I was there. You know I don't play when it comes to my favorite girl."

I smirked and rolled my eyes. Got into character a little bit for my number one customer. "Yeah, they were definitely on some bullshit. I'm not allowed to go back until I pay the fine."

"Well what's the fine?"

"Half a stack."

"Oh, well shit, girl you shoulda been found a way to get at me. Where that nigga you got? Why you got him for and you still banned from the club? His business running bad or some shit? He shoulda been supplied you with that."

"Nah, he…he'd rather not see me dancing in the club. You know how that goes. He's glad I can't go back."

"Well is he keeping you paid? I know you got bills and shit."

"Why you think I look so mean today? I got a lot of shit to figure out. Bills included."

Dougie picked up a menu and shook his head. "That ain't right. I do business with the owner over there all the time. Want me to go handle that?"

"If you can, why not? I need to make my money. You know I stay focused on my paper."

This was all going in the right direction. Dash would be mad as hell if he knew I was a foot back in the door, but he'd get over it eventually. I needed to do this for me. Especially with this waitress interview lingering over my head, I was feeling kind of desperate. Shit just got better and better, though.

"Man, fuck that. I'ma give you something that dude can't argue with." Dougie reached in his pocket and pulled out a fat wad of cash, which I was all too used to when dealing with him. He peeled off an assload of twenties and handed it to me. "Ay, count that and let me know how much it is. I'm 'bout to put my order in."

The cash counted up to four hundred and twenty dollars. I told him, and he gave me four more twenties like it was nothing. The roll of dough he stuffed back into his pocket was still a pretty good size. Right on time, my order was finished. Dougie offered to pay for it, but I'd already paid for the food back when I ordered it. So instead, he gave me the change from his food and sent me off with a wink.

"Make ya' money sweetheart. I'll see you tonight."

I walked out the Chinese restaurant with a new attitude, hot food, and a beaming smile. Dougie was my motherfucking best customer ever.

14

I wasn't expecting Dash to call me, and I didn't call or text him at all. I was packing my bags to go to work, and the last thing I needed was for him to come through trying to stop me. I prayed to God he didn't decide to just show up at my door. I was going to the club a little earlier than usual just to get up in there before he could find out. I called Kaycee and asked for a ride and kept her up to date on the plan. I felt like a fugitive escaping to Strokers.

She came through around ten and I was ready as soon as she pulled up. The second I was in the car and we hit the street, my phone vibrated and Dash's name and picture flashed on the screen.

"Girl, *fuck*. I hope he's not pulling up to my house or nothing. It won't take him long to put two and two together."

Kaycee flicked on her turn signal and her shoulders bobbed with laughter. "You cutting it real close. You know he goes to the strip club all the damn time. He just might see you in there, anyway."

"Well at least I'll have the chance to get up in there and make some money first."

"How mad do you think he would be?"

"Pretty fucking hot. But not leave me on my own and stop fucking with me hot. He'll be okay, I promise you."

"You sure about this?"

I thought about the interview at Chili's. "Hell yeah. The sooner I'm in my heels, the happier I'll be."

The anxious feelings in my stomach and the urgency in my chest melted away after I paid Ron and ducked off into the dressing room. Shit was good to go. It was still fairly early as far as the crowd was concerned, so at least for now I wouldn't have to worry about sneaking around the club. Dash usually hit the club around one in the morning or later.

Still, there were a few early birds in the place who flocked to me while I made use of the empty, smaller stage in the corner. I was just warming up, but them young niggas was enjoying the show.

By time the first group of dudes walked away, I had at least sixty dollars at my feet. I was good at looking at an amount of money, whether it be spread out or in a neat stack and estimating the right number. I had raked up over a hundred by the time it was eleven. Still kind of slow if you asked me, but I knew that the real money usually came in around the same time Dash would…if he was coming. I was crossing my fingers that the only person I'd see tonight was Dougie. If he showed up, I was going to make at least eight hundred tonight or better. I had enough of the small stage and needed something to drink, so I made sure I picked my money up this time, and went to the bar for a pineapple and cranberry juice.

Bubbles – the one who'd brought me water the night I was kicked out – nudged me in the shoulder.

"I see you made it back. Red ain't been back yet."

"Sucks to be her," was my curt response.

She chuckled. "And I ain't gon' tell you how Brooklyn ass tried to fly under the radar but you know word spread. She wasn't here more than an hour and got her ass kicked out *and* her fine doubled. Ron don't play."

"Yeah that was stupid of her. She shouldn't have started a fight if she knew she was that broke."

"Exactly."

Bubbles and I stood leaned up at the bar without words and just vibed along with the DJ for a moment. She was cool enough so I decided to ask her.

"Ay, Bubbles. Do you ever see Dash in here? You know who Dash is right?"

"Girl, we all know who Dash is. Yeah. He be in here like every other night. Why?"

"You just using a figure of speech, or he really be up in here like every other night, literally?"

"Uh…I mean he never here too long but he do come and show his face every now and then. What's up?"

"Nothing, really. If you see him just find me and let me know, if you not with a customer, though."

Bubbles nodded. "Gotcha, ma."

"Thanks." She was the coolest chick in the club. I'd never had a problem with her. In fact, we even hung out once or twice outside the club on some homegirl type shit. I knew her real name, too. It was Berissa. Or Bernetta. Something to that effect.

I left my empty cup on the bar and asked if she had gum. She broke me off a piece before I went and changed my outfit. I changed outfits anywhere from four to six times a night.

When I came out, I felt a light tug on my wrist. Hairs on the back of my neck stood straight, and I turned around slowly. Before I could even focus my eyes on the face behind me, dollar bills flew up and rained all around like confetti.

"She's back, she's back!" Dougie stood leaned up to a table with a smile, and as always, a fat stack of ones. "Pick up ya money, ma. We don't want any repeats."

I grinned and bent down to collect what was mine. Dougie was here early compared to usual, but unlike usual he was here alone. Or at least I didn't see the rest of his crew. They always rolled tight to him like a security blanket. Bright or any of them niggas were nowhere to be seen. It didn't matter to me, long as their MVP was in attendance.

He requested a private room and in gratitude from earlier I made sure I gave him one hell of a show. I had him back there pressed up against the wall and backed it up completely in the nude. I let him fondle my breasts a little. They were sore but he was so gentle it didn't even matter. It was kind of turning me on, even. I placed Dash's face on his body and fantasized just to make the dance even more personal. Personal meant more money. He was already done with the stack he came in here with and was digging his pockets for more. He didn't bother to change out the twenties out of his pants pocket. He started throwing them, whole. I looked down to the ground. At least twelve hundred and counting. It was like a sea of money. I wouldn't be surprised if Dougie came just to give it to me and leave. The way his boys didn't show up with him made me feel like that was exactly the case. He'd shown up exclusively to pay me some attention, and shit, to just pay me.

Coming back to the club was turning out to be the best shit to happen to me this entire week.

Dougie sat down on the little bench and I climbed up the wall and put my leg up. Let him get a planetarium view of the kitten. I could tell he was about to slob on himself so I climbed back down, played around in his lap, and let his hardness rub me through his jeans. Dougie let all the money in his hand go and took a deep breath.

"You got me back here embarrassed. I done fucked up and ran out of money."

I shrugged. "You've done enough for me today. You good. I got you for another song if you want."

"Nah, I can't stay. I'm supposed to be out handling something but I snuck up in here to see you. I can't explain what you do to a nigga, man. You the best, baddest, thickest muh'fucka in here. You already know that, though."

I shrugged. "Being humble is a virtue. I think."

He smiled and moved my bang out my face. "Nah, it's cool. Pick up ya money and ya clothes. You good for now. Meet me out in the front and I'll buy you a drink before I go."

I thought up an excuse to turn his drink down so not as to seem rude. "I wasn't feeling well earlier so I took some painkillers. A drink isn't what I should be on right now, but I appreciate it."

"Ay, hope you don't mind me asking, but is that nigga treating you right?"

"Excuse me?"

"Ay, this ain't even much me. I hate niggas who be on some bitch shit, some hatin' shit. I ain't tryna be a hatin' nigga, but I see some shit, and I just be thinking to myself, ya dig? Just wondering if he holding you down. Nigga be in here even on nights you wasn't in this bitch, but yet and still he couldn't break you off to get you back in here working? I'm just saying, I could do you better than that. Everyone know you got a nigga. We know that's ya dude. But you seem like you deserve something a little better. As you can see," he looked down at all the money I had yet to pick up, covering the floor and making it impossible to catch a glimpse of the carpet. Nothing else had to be said. I was flattered, but from the outside looking in, he didn't quite understand that there was a complex set of circumstances holding Dash and I together.

I looked at Dougie. Through the black lights and the rough exterior, I actually felt like he cared for me more than I gave him credit for. He was good for his money, but I wasn't really looking to take him seriously on his offer. I continued to rake up my money and politely declined.

"Thanks Dougie, but Dash and I just have a few things we need to work on. Other than that we're good. We've been working at it for a year and he's not perfect, but he's good to me. Thanks for the concern, though. I appreciate everything you do for me. I really do. Don't think I'm tryna play you or nothing."

I mean, that was the ropes. I just needed his money. Besides, he was probably just experiencing what some of us dancers call "T-Pain Syndrome". He was in love with a stripper. I did nothing to seek his interest other than just being good at my job. At the end of the day, this *was* just a job.

Dougie nodded and accepted the reality of it. For just a split second, he seemed defeated, but he shook it off, stood up, and left the private room.

I finished stuffing the money into my bag and walked out the private room naked, clothes in hand, with a choice to make. I'd made so much in the back I could just tip out early and leave, or I could change outfits again and try to push for two thousand tonight.

A hand grabbed my wrist again and I turned around in character, ready to throw my seduction back at Dougie if he found more money to spend. Instead stood Dash, staring my naked ass up and down with the fire of the sun in his eyes. I swallowed hard and readied myself for the heat he was 'bout to bring down on me. I guess I had no choice but to just call it a night after all.

15

"Get in the fucking car, Tonnie."

"I'm trying. I dropped my bag, damn."

I felt eyes on me so I searched the parking lot and seen a nigga two rows over watching the two of us closely.

"Ay, who the fuck is that? What the fuck a nigga fuckin' lookin' at?" I looked over and Tonnie was still over there with the car door open, standing outside. "Tonnie, get in the fucking car."

"Dash, shut up! I'm trying to find my keys! I think they slid under the car."

"Ay, hurry the fuck up. I can't fucking believe you, man. I can't fucking..." I groaned and slammed my driver's side door, gripping the steering wheel until my hands turned blue. Shit like this was how niggas with low tolerance ended up hitting a female. There was only the one time, but fully sober, I would never put my hands on Tonnie like that. Tonight, though, she had me on edge. If not for Kaycee, I'd be the lost nigga right now. Ignorant to the fact that my girl was back in the club swinging her naked ass around. I looked through the windshield. Same dude was standing in the distance leaned up on his truck. All eyes my way. "Ay, what the fuck is wrong wit' dis nigga?" I mumbled to myself.

Tonnie finally got her shit and sat in the car. I could cut her attitude with a knife. She was the one who snuck behind my back and she had the nerve to be mad?

"Where the fuck you got the money, Tonnie? I know you didn't dip into your car money to go back to the club. Where the fuck you got it from? Don't bullshit me."

"No I didn't dip into my fucking car money. By the way, I'll be pushing my own shit by next week. I got all the money I need."

"YOU COULDA BEEN HAD ALL THE MONEY YOU

NEED!" I lost it and yelled at her. "I don't understand why the FUCK you feel like you need to be up in the fucking club, man. I TOLD YOU I didn't want you back in there and FIRST CHANCE YOU FUCKING GET I catch yo' NAKED ASS coming out the back? Man when the fuck did we start on some sneaky lying type bullshit, shawd'? What the fuck were you thinkin' Tonnie? That a nigga wouldn't find out?"

I was careful to whip around to the row the nosy nigga was standing in and rolled by real slow. His head followed the car and stopped when I did, right in front of him. I rolled the window down. I saw his face and I saw the Tahoe. Niggas around my way were familiar. I knew who he was. And especially his regards to Tonnie inside the club on a regular basis. It all made sense.

"We got a problem, boy?"

Dougie lifted his shirt up and the handle of his glock shined under the parking lot lamps. "Same shit I'm tryna figure out," he said.

I nodded with a frown and pulled off. From that point on, nigga was on my hit list. Tonnie definitely couldn't go within a mile radius of Strokers now cuz ol' boy loved himself some Tonnie. I didn't need that nigga in her face, ever.

"You see? You got niggas all in our business and shit. I'm telling you now, that shit is finna get ugly. I don't need to ever run into that mothafucka. You don't need to be back around this bitch, Tonnie. I'm telling you that now. You go back to Strokers and that's the fucking end of it."

She nodded, but she wouldn't look at me. "You think this a joke? I'm serious as fuck!" She finally looked at me with tears falling from her face. "What the fuck *you* crying for? You knew I would be mad. Don't tell me you ain't know I was finna be mad, man. Keep them fucking tears, man. I don't buy that shit at all. Matta fact, you still ain't answer me 'bout the money. Where you got it from?"

She refused to answer. She just wiped her tears silently and kept looking out the window. I wasn't going to let this shit go that easy. "You tryin' a nigga, man. If you ain't take it from the money you been saving, and I ain't give it to you, how you come up on half a stack overnight? Who gave you the money?"

"Dougie gave it to me."

I damn near slammed the brakes to that answer. "What the FUCK? That nigga? What the FUCK HE DOING.....man, *see*? You tryna get a nigga locked up. That's exactly what you...TONNIE YOU TRYIN THE SHIT OUT A NIGGA MAN!" I couldn't even get my thoughts out. She was trying to make niggas go crazy. Times like this I wished I still did bitches like I did before Shakima. When I didn't see shit 'bout a female other than pussy. Having a kid made a nigga feel some type of respect to bitches that deserved it, but this one. Man, she was 'bout to lose mine.

"You fucking him?"

"What?"

"Oh, now you know how to talk. I said are you fucking him?"

"Dash, you are taking this *way* too far! I'm sorry I went to the club, alright. I'll stay home from now on or go get a real fucking job. Whatever you want, I'll meet you halfway, but now you're the one trying me. Don't you FUCKING ask me that!"

"YA'LL FUCKING YES OR NO?"

Her tears came double time and she started bouncing her leg up and down. I was pissing her off, but fuck it. She needed to answer the question. She wouldn't give me an answer.

"Tonnie, ay, for real. I'm not playing with you, man. You been fucking him? And if so how long? Cuz that nigga be feelin' you up in the club like he know that body from somewhere. He do that shit in my face, too. I ain't never said nothing, but I don't know a nigga who pay a bitch outside the club unless he getting something in return. Fuck that, you need to make sure that baby is mine."

Once I said that, it was like she turned into a black cat and could scratch my eyes right out my head. She went off. Started screaming and shouting at me, slamming her hand on the dashboard, pushing a nigga in his head and shit, crying, and more screaming.

I didn't say shit else because I felt like I'd pulled a sensitive nerve and real talk, if she would've answered me in the first place, I would have never asked. I didn't have any more questions. I pulled up in front her apartment and asked her to get the fuck out of my car.

16

Kenny and I were laid up in the bed after he blessed me with some mind-bending, backbone breaking sex. It didn't get better than him. I was convinced.

He held me up to his chest and I held him tightly around the waist under the sheets. I was almost knocked out in a post-orgasmic kind of way when my phone buzzed. It was under the pillow somewhere. Kenny and I lifted our heads and searched for it. I missed the call, but seeing that it was Tonnie, I dialed her right back. It had to be like, two something in the morning. I didn't even glimpse at the time before I redialed her number.

"Hello?"

"Ginger where are you at?"

"I'm at home, why?"

"Because. I need someone here. I don't want to be alone. Dash really pissed me off and I'm not thinking like myself. I don't want to be here alone. Can you get over here? I know the buses stopped running, but, but please. Ginger can you make it over here?"

I sat straight up. "Tonnie, what's going on? Are you safe? You okay? Where is he? What's the matter?"

"He..." She attempted to tell the story but the only word I understood was "he". Everything else was swallowed by tears and came out as gibberish.

"Tonnie, look, try and calm down. You don't need to be worked up like this, okay? It's bad for the baby. Just try and calm down until I can figure out how to get there."

"I don't want this fucking baby. I want an abortion. Fuck the interview. That's what I'm doing tomorrow. I'm getting this shit taken out of me. I swear."

"*Whoa*…whoa. Okay, I see what you mean. You're not thinking clearly. Tonnie, I'll be right over and stop thinking like that. We'll talk this out. Give me a minute, I'll be there soon."

By the time I hung up, Kenny was hanging onto my every word. He looked confused. In a few words I filled him in. "My sister is panicking about something and I can't even understand her. I need to get there. How can we get there?" I found myself being a little panicked as well. I had to calm down and think for a second. Kenny's cousin had got dropped off to pick up his ride hours ago and there was no longer free transportation. First thought was to my roommate. "Let me see if Asia is in her room and can drop us to Tonnie's house."

I went and knocked on Asia's door and although a TV light was flicking through the crack under the door, she didn't answer. She was probably sleeping, but this was an emergency. I went back to my phone and called her. Still no answer. Then I heard her bedroom door open so I darted back out into the living room. Asia was standing in her doorway looking half dead.

"What…is everything okay?" She grumbled.

"Asia. I need a huge favor from you. Can you *please* take me by my sister's? Can you drop me off? You don't even have to worry about me getting back. I'm so sorry. I know what time it is. My sister is pregnant and she's going through some type of crisis right now. I have to get there somehow."

Asia looked really uncomfortable, really quick. I could tell she was extremely reluctant at just the thought of leaving the house.

"Look, don't worry about it. I'm sorry I bothered you, Asia. I'll Uber it. I'm just panicking." Even in my panic, I still wanted to avoid the $25 ride, but if it was necessary…

Now she looked like her conscience was tugging at her and making her feel bad. "Hold on." She sighed and turned around for her bedroom. Two seconds later she came back and tossed me the keys. "Please, please be careful, Ginger. I wouldn't be able to explain to my mom if anything happened to the car. Make it back before eight cuz I got class," she yawned.

"Asia, thank you soooooo much. Thank you, I swear I owe you

something."

"Just put a ten in the tank or something," she said from behind the closing bedroom door.

Kenny was already dressed when I went back into the room and after I threw something on real quick, we were heading out the door. I called Tonnie and asked if she needed anything. Although she said no, I stopped at Steak N' Shake and picked up a cookies and cream shake – her favorite – in hopes that it would cheer her up. Since we were now closer to where Kenny lived I went ahead and dropped him off, in the back of my mind a little reluctant that our night had to end this way.

Tonnie had big puffy eyes when I arrived, but she wasn't crying. Guess she'd gotten all her tears out. It seemed like she was now in anger mode, if anything. I just wanted to know what happened.

"Can you believe Dash had the nerve to ask me if this baby was his?" she dug into the shake and savored it for a second, then continued. I was too shocked to say anything. Fury was rising in the core of my chest for that excuse of a man.

"I went back to the club. Yeah, that was on me. I was wrong for that. But I damn sure made money and I'm not sorry about that. This nigga caught me and yanked me out the club, then gonna ask if I'm fucking around on him."

I looked over my shoulder to hide my angst from Tonnie. I was disappointed in Tonnie for going back to that strip club, but that was halfway expected from her stubborn ass. This nigga Dash was a whole other subject. He needed someone to straighten his ass out.

"Did he manhandle you?"

"I don't think so. That's not even on my mind. I'm just trying to figure out how to get out of this situation. I'm not ready to be nobody's mother and definitely not for some asshole who basically thinks I'm a hoe anyway and would talk to me any type of way. I need to take care of this problem. I don't want to be pregnant anymore. Somehow he thinking it ain't his anyway, so fuck it."

I took a deep breath and thought of a way to get into her head and persuade her otherwise. "Tonnie, can I talk to you, no bullshit, for a moment?"

She didn't say anything, but just followed my question with a big scoop of oreo shake. "What."

"You know what," I said, wiping my hands down my face. "No one is really ready to be a parent but shit happens and you have to take on responsibility, Tonnie. I'm upset you went back, but the important part is, whether he disrespected you or not, you can't just make the situation go away and run from the problem. You don't know how this baby will affect your life. You might need this. Everything has its purpose. And I'm not just throwing a bunch of cliché shit at you, but I'm just being for real. Don't just drop the issue and think that's going to make it all better. Baby or not, Dash is an asshole, and the baby doesn't need to suffer for ya'll two getting into it. I can't tolerate that. You shouldn't, either."

She sat on her bed the whole time, holding her shake with both hands, staring into the carpet.

"Tonnie, you listening? Can you say something?"

Tears trickled down her face and into her lap. "He hurt my feelings so bad. I love him, G. I know I hurt him the way I went about it, but he didn't have to take it there. That was so fucked up. I just…It doesn't seem like real life. I wake up every day reminding myself that I have a baby on the way and I be scared as shit because I wasn't planning this. I don't know where I'm going, much less how I'll be as a mother. I take care of myself but taking care of a kid, that's a whole other thing…and for Dash to just be on and off the way he is…this is all fucked up. All fucked up."

A lump of sand was rising in my throat at the sight of her so distraught. I grabbed sister in a bear hug. "Tonnie, it's going to be a challenge, but I'm here to help you. Mommy is there for you. So is Dad. You have family. You can't do it all by yourself. You're always trying, but you don't have to. We will be here no matter what. Just don't give up on it. I want a niece or nephew and whenever it gets too hard for you, I'll come take over. If it's anything like you, you know it's gonna be hard-headed and bad as hell. You know this," I nudged her with a smile and we laughed for a second despite our need of tissues.

She sniffled. "G, you have no idea how this is, or what you're talking about for real. But thanks. I love you." We hugged again, and I was put at ease to see her take a long breath and relax.

"Is your shake melting? It's hot as hell in here. Damn, is the AC on in this bitch?"

Tonnie nodded. "I feel it. Don't know about you. I'm actually cold."

"Weird ass pregnant people," I grinned.

Tonnie flipped me a bird before going to put her treat in the freezer for later. I wasn't sure about her mental state, but at least she wasn't freaking out anymore.

17

Kaycee brought me a plate of scrambled eggs, grits, and sausage links. She set a cold glass of grape juice on the table and put the remote by my plate.

"I'm about to dress my kids for school. Make yourself comfortable."

She disappeared to the back and left me to myself. I felt all kinds of wrong about being there, but if Tonnie was really sliding with that other nigga, revenge was bittersweet.

Kaycee was walking around the place in an oversized T-shirt, nothing on her ass but purple panties. She whizzed back out and crossed me to her laundry room, power walked her son into the bathroom, zoomed her daughter into the kitchen to fix her a bowl of cereal, and then got her son out the shower and carried him back to the back room. I was finished with my plate almost as soon as she sat it down, but when she'd finally got both her kids in the kitchen to eat, she came back to me in the sun room and took my empty plate.

"Want more?"

"Thanks, but nah. That was enough."

She smiled, satisfied with herself and nodded. Turned around and swayed her ass back to the kitchen. She put an extra dip in her walk and glanced at me over her shoulder with a grin.

Looking at her ass hanging out them draws, I was wondering to myself if push came to shove, would I actually fuck my girl's best friend for the sake of getting even. I knew I was definitely capable since the bitch was basically begging for it, but I wasn't sure if that's the type of nigga I wanted to be. A few years ago, it wouldn't take a second thought, but I was trying to grow the fuck up and leave that shit behind me. I was mad at Tonnie and all, but what if it was really nothing. More than likely, that baby was definitely mine. Nah, fucking Kaycee would be taking things too far. If it happened, I wouldn't be able to take it back.

She came back from the kitchen and sat next to me on the sofa. She put a hand on my knee. "You good? Feelin' better?"

I nodded. I was feeling uncomfortable again. I didn't even want to be there anymore. I thought that Kaycee was tacky for having some new nigga at her house with her kids there, walking around half dressed and shit. If I ever found out Shakima was carrying on like that in front of Quantrell, I'd definitely be at her fucking throat.

Then I thought about the way I found out about Tonnie last night. I was so mad that I didn't stop to think. The way this bitch had been trying to get at me lately, all this shit coulda been a part of some type of fucked up plan to get me in this exact mind state that would lead me to her fucking door. I decided to test her out a little bit to see what she would say.

"Ay, you took Tonnie up to the club, right? Why ain't you tell her no when she asked you? You know like I do that she pregnant and shit."

"That's my girl and all, but shit, you can't tell her no sometimes. She stubborn as hell. Dancing is her life. She gon' always be a stripper, if you ask me. You can't help someone who don't wanna do better with themselves. It's like a lost cause. But I mean, I know it's not good for her. Why you think I called you? Someone needed to go get her in check."

Damn, she was a real shiesty bitch. "You coulda put her in check and told her you weren't gonna drop her ass off. You can't play both sides."

"You right." She sat back and focused on the TV screen. "Ya'll finna kiss and make up, huh?"

"I wouldn't say that just yet. Since you like to keep a nigga informed and shit just tell me this. She ever mention a nigga named Dougie to you? She ever say anything about being with him?"

She looked confused, genuinely. "Honest to God, I have no idea who that is."

I took that as an honest answer. If Kaycee nosy ass had never heard of him, chances are Tonnie never had a reason to mention him, so either she was playing this real low key, or I was wrong as hell.

"You think she fucking someone else? Damn, she on it like

that?"

I was irritated with how easy it was for her to set up and bad mouth someone who trusted her so much, and someone you couldn't trust would lie, cheat, and steal. I definitely didn't need to be here.

"Mommy, we're done."

Her son and daughter came out holding their empty bowls in their hands, staring their little nosy eyes at me the whole time. I waited for Kaycee to go tend to her kids so they would get up out of my face. I shouldn't have even been there around them. That part irked me the most.

She got up and took them in the back to clean them up and then they came out to put on their shoes. She at least had some jeans on when she came out the room this time.

"I'm taking them to school. You wanna stay or you got somewhere to be?" She smiled seductively when the kids weren't looking.

I stood up and grabbed my phone without a word. Before I walked out the front door and passed the children putting on their bookbags, I turned to her with the straight face and said, "Ay Kaycee, erase my number from your phone and leave me the fuck alone."

18

After Ginger left, I took a nap. She talked me back into going for the new job later on, and I needed to get rest so I would be refreshed for the interview. I woke to my phone going off. The screen read "Bernessa". It took me a while to connect the dots in my brain because for a second I had no idea who that even was. When I picked up and said hello, the voice matched a face in my brain.

"Hey, this is Sunshine, right? Or, Tonnie. Whatever."

"Yeah." I yawned and wiped my eyes out. "Hey, Bubbles."

"Oh okay," she laughed. "Ain't called you in a minute. Wasn't sure if your number was the same."

"Yeah, it's me. What's up?"

"You was sleep? My bad, girl. Look, my fault to bother you but someone asked me to pass along a message."

"What you talkin' about?"

"Dougie. He came back in the club last night after you left. I gave him a dance or whatever and he asked me if I was cool with you. He wanted to find a way to get in touch with you outside the workplace. Apparently your number one customer doesn't have your number."

"Cuz that shit went bad for me once, and I don't give it out in the club no more." I groaned as I sat up and stretched. It was about that time for me to get up and start getting ready for Ginger to come by, anyway.

"He gave me his info to give to you. He wants you to call him."

I sighed and recounted all the events from last night. He was probably upset about the whole Dash thing. He never outright searched me out before. His effort to pick things up outside my job was coming out of nowhere. After getting in trouble with Dash, I didn't think communication with Dougie was what I really needed.

Bubbles said she'd text his number to me and asked me if I was coming back later that night.

"Nah, I made it good yesterday. I'm set for a couple days." Ultimately, there was no such thing but I had to say something reasonable.

"Must be nice," she said. "I got too many bills past due. I shoulda never went out to California and went shopping like that. My oldest brother stays out there."

"Mm Hmm." I was tuning her out at that point, still trying to figure out what Dougie's true intentions were. I wanted to make shit right with Dash, but shit, if he kept tripping, Dougie could be my next resort. When my belly starts to get big that would open up a whole new conversation between us. I'm sure that shit would end before it could even get a good chance to start. In that case, I was probably better off just staying where I was. By the time I brushed my thoughts aside and tuned back in, Bubbles was telling me about her homegirl's party at this club called Drip City and how she was getting paid to be the go-go dancer for the night. When she was done explaining her side hustles, we ended conversation and I got up out of bed and into the shower.

Ginger showed up by the time I'd changed outfits three or four times, and with her advice, I ended up just changing right back into the fit I put on first. She had me looking semi-professional in khaki capris, a peach-colored cardigan, and brown slip on heels. Low heels, though. Probably two or three inches off the ground. We would be taking the bus over to the restaurant, so I wasn't trying to do it up with pumps or anything of that nature. I was nervous about not having a resume and shit, but she insisted that this job would be a surefire snatch.

"If he doesn't hire you, you either really really suck as a candidate, or he's a fucking liar, and I'd bet anyone any amount of money that the first option is not the case."

"If I'm supposed to be getting this shit automatically, what's the point of the interview?"

"I don't know, Tonnie. I guess just to keep things legit. But don't worry about it. You're a pretty woman and your cleavage is poppin'. He's a guy. He's gonna definitely hire you looking like that. I wouldn't be worried 'bout a stupid piece of paper. Everything he'll be interested in will be sitting right in front of him."

"Wow," I locked the door behind us on the way out the apartment. "Look at my little sister pimping me out. So does he really give you that kind of vibe? Like a perv' or something?"

She shrugged. "Nah, not a perv', just a man. He was already giving me the goofy smile when I was talking to him about you. I told him I had a sister and his attitude was more or less like shit, bring her! He'd probably like to hire us both." She stopped suddenly, halfway down the stairs. "You have your ID and social card on you right? I'd be prepared just in case he has you do the paperwork all in one shot."

"All in my wallet. Let's walk fast because it's already a quarter after. I'll be surprised if we don't miss the bus."

The commute wasn't bad. My feet could stand it. Wasn't too much walking once we got off the bus, either. I was hungry as hell, but I wasn't going to pay attention to it. I had to remain focused. It took us a good ten minutes to get there but once we walked inside, the scents of different foods clashed and hit me like a brick wall. Made me feel sick-like despite the fact that my stomach was rumbling. Ginger went to request the manager and the hostess sat us at a booth and served us each a drink on the house. Ginger asked for an iced tea and I was so grateful to sip on some ice water. If not for the ice water, it felt like I was going to fall out.

The manager's name was Greggory. He was cool. He let Ginger sit at the bar and offered for her to order any appetizer she wanted, free of charge. I could tell she'd appreciate me getting a job here as long as she could continue to receive free food. That was something I didn't think about. I guess I'd appreciate free food once in a while my damn self.

Once Greggory and I were at the bar alone, he had me fill out a basic application and asked me a few questions about my customer service experience, my schedule, any other obligations. Everything was cool until he asked me about reliable transportation. I was hesitant to let him know that my car was actually in the shop, so I lied and told him I was driving. It wasn't a full lie. All bullshit aside I was looking to have my car out by that next weekend which was the last weekend in the month. By next month I would be riding myself around once again, so I didn't feel bad about telling a small fib if it was what I had to do to keep from being exed out of an opportunity.

Ginger was absolutely right. Greggory could barely read through my application *and* keep his eyes off of me. Just like she'd said, this interview seemed like a bunch of bullshit just for the record because he nodded once we were all done and extended his hand with a smile that said his mind had long been made up.

"If you don't mind giving me the pleasure of being your manager, we can shake on it and I'll bring you some papers to fill out so you can get started here."

That was too easy. I grinned and took his hand firmly to seal the deal. Soon as he disappeared, Ginger leaned back from the bar and we exchanged winks and thumbs up. I was absolutely against coming to do this, but my little sister was right most of the time. This time was no exception. She hooked a bitch up for real. Suddenly, I didn't feel so bad about myself for pulling in a real job.

19

I kicked back once I got back to my place and relaxed. After I finished up the papers with Greggory, he gave me my first schedule to come in for training, and then allowed me to order something for free, as well. So my hunger was settled, and I was in a great mood. Ginger was still with me, and she was down for relaxing. The second she hit the couch she'd balled up and fell into a deep sleep almost immediately. I took that opportunity to go roll a bidi. I lit it up in my bedroom with the window open and a can of air freshener at my side. I didn't need Ginger giving me hell about my relaxation methods.

Just when I was leaned back, puffing slowly, Ginger busted into the room with the evil eye. I almost jumped into the ceiling. She startled the hell out of me.

"Tonnie, I *know* you are not."

I looked at the can of Glade I'd been spraying like it was full of shit.

"Are you serious right now? You're smoking? That doesn't smell like weed. What is that?"

"Spices, G. Damn. Fucking spices."

"Does it matter? I don't think any type of smoking is safe when you're pregnant. You're tripping!"

"You're not a doctor, Ginger. Leave me alone."

She sat on the bed next to me with an attitude. "Let me see it."

I looked at her crazy. "No."

"I'm not going to throw it away. Let me see it."

"You tryna smoke on it? Roll your own."

I handed her a ziploc bag and she grabbed it up and held it in the light. Opened it up and took a whiff. "This shit looks like potpourri…but it smells like…cloves and…a fuckin' spice rack. What kind of effect does it give you."

"Nothing really. Just a laid back sensation. No high like weed, but it takes the edge off your day like a cigarette. It's soothing."

"So what is it called?"

"A bidi."

"Where you got it from?"

"The Indian market by the club. You'd be surprised what you can find in there."

"Interesting. Let me try it."

I handed it to her and the second it hit her fingers she bolted out the room. "Ginger! Quit!" I chased her into the kitchen and back out into the living room. She zoomed out the front door and when I followed her and hit the corner, she was holding it over the banister.

"How old are you? Why you got me chasing you? Give it back."

"I don't like you smoking, Tonnie. You need to quit."

"It doesn't do anything to the baby. C'mon, Ginger, quit playing."

"I don't trust it." She dropped it on the ground one story down and I wanted to smack her head off her shoulders. I couldn't believe she just did that. I stomped in the house and went to protect my stash before she caught herself trying to throw that away, too. I hid the baggie behind my bed. When the front door opened and closed, I counted backward from ten to one. Up until then I was having a good day with her. Sometimes she acted like we were twelve and five all over again and irritated me to no end.

She came through the bedroom door with a smile, dusting her hands off on her legs. "My niece or nephew will thank me later. Love you."

"Yeah, whatever the fuck ever. Get out."

She jumped on me and hugged the air out of my lungs, sat her whole body in my lap and had me cradling her like a child. "Ginger. Get. OFF." I couldn't help but laugh at her silliness.

"Kenny's taking me to the Drake concert tomorrow."

"What? That's cool. Sounds fun. Where ya'll sitting?"

"Fifth row. Floor seats."

"Oh, what? For real? How he handled that? Kenny don't look like the type to have money like that."

"Can I tell you a secret? But you can't tell anyone. Like, we gotta pinky promise. Old school."

I shrugged and locked pinkies. Not like any of Kenny's business would even be interesting enough to repeat, but just to make her feel better, I swore.

"I don't know exactly what they got him doing, but he's mixed up in the hustle game. I don't know what or who he deals with, what his supply is or none of that. But he's getting paid. See my nails, and my fresh ass HD lace? He did all of that. Completely spoiled me."

I'll admit, I was surprised. "Wow, look at you. Got a little nerd hustler keeping you fresh and don't know how to act."

"Shut up. I didn't even know. I would never have guessed but he was throwing out money and I was just like um…Kenny, you don't have a job."

I laughed. "Well shit, a hustler with a degree is better than a hustler with no plans for himself. That's what I'm talking about…don't be me, be better than me. I'm happy for you. I meant to tell you that. It seems like you and Kenny have a strong thing going. I like seeing ya'll together. He treats you good."

She nodded. "Yeah…and I need to be careful before I let his sexy ass get me knocked up. No offense but I can't deal wit' something like that…it's just that oh my *God*, Tonnie. The D is soooooo good!"

"Eww. Let's not go there, Sis." I laughed but I was serious. She was still the baby of the two of us. I remembered the day she was born and I did *not* want to picture details of my little sister getting it beat in.

"Well, to get back to the other subject, tell ya boy to be careful out there. These niggas don't play about they money, and the cops don't play about these niggas."

She nodded. "Yeah. I want to know more, but at the same time I don't. I'ma just let him do him. As long as he stays in school, that's his choice."

"Get off, Ginger. I gotta pee."

I went to the bathroom and came back, Ginger's whole mood was upside down. She was holding my phone, looking down at it and scrolling through something. I wanted to ask what was wrong, but I just walked up and took my phone away.

"What's this? Why you readin' my texts?"

"You gotta be fucking kidding me."

"Wait…what….what the fuck?"

I went through the text messages my nosy sister had already opened and was losing my cool word by word. I couldn't believe the content of the messages much less the name and number they were coming from. There must've been a mix up…she was talking about someone else's nigga. Wait no. She said his name. Right nigga. Definitely the right nigga. I was in shock.

Ginger cracked her hands and ran her fingers through her hair. Looked like she was the one whose best friend was tryna fuck her boyfriend. She popped her lips and gazed out the window. "So what do we need to do? You don't need to be fighting again, so just point me in her direction. I never felt right about that woman. Where do I need to go to set her ass straight?"

"Put your shoes on. Let's go."

"Nah, you can stay here. She expecting you to show up. Just let me handle it, Tonnie."

"Ginger, shut up. Put your shoes on. Let's go."

She threw her hands up in the air. "Fuck it, I'm just saying. I'm down."

"Well less talking, please. I can't take anything else right now. Let's go."

20

I had Ginger wait outside the shop. When I walked in, the owner was sitting up at the front desk watching the 6 o'clock news on Fox. She barely looked up, but she saw my face and greeted me.

"Hey, Tonnie."

"What's up, Yvette. Kaycee here?"

"She probably doin' her last head in there. Go and see."

"Thank you."

Once I turned the corner and Kaycee caught sight of me, her stance became stiff and she looked away before we could lock eyes for real. She sighed, rolled her eyes, and continued pressing her customer's short Fantasia-like hairstyle. She didn't say anything, and continued pretending I wasn't standing there. There was only one more customer other than the one in her chair, and from under the hair dryer, her eyes bounced between the both of us. She could sense that something rotten was cooking in the air.

"Kaycee?"

"Tonnie."

"So this is what we on now? You known me this long and a little jealousy is all it takes to pull out your true colors?"

She took the iron out of her customer's hair before looking at me like I was the one fucked up. "Jealous? You think you have anything worth being jealous over?"

"Why yes. Yes I do. I can make what you make in a month in one night, and I have a man that can make what you make in a month in one hour. I think you're sneaky, you're fucked up, you're spiteful, and you deserve your ass whooped, but most of all I feel sorry for you because all of that just comes from the fact that you're just lonely. And jealous."

She set the iron back in its little oven holder and sighed. "A moment outside. Now."

With a grin I extended my arm as to say *you first*, knowing that Ginger was already waiting outside for her. If she thought she was about to pull a trick on me, she had another thing coming. I followed her out the door and her steps slowed down when she hit the sidewalk. She must've spotted my sister leaned up against her black piece of shit car.

"So you have no more use for our friendship because what now? I need to hear this from your mouth cuz it doesn't make too much sense."

"Because. You won't ever be shit and I'm tryna move on and surround myself with goal-oriented people. You don't have shit going for yourself and you have never had a desire to go to school or get a real job. You take everything for granted and you're exhausting to be around. I can't take it anymore."

Ginger kept her arms crossed, looking at me instead of Kaycee and I already knew why. Ginger was extremely protective of me. If she landed eyes on that bitch, she was going to swing.

"And I guess when you say goal-oriented you mean goals like steal your best friend's man."

She chuckled like I told a joke. "I don't think you understand. *You* been hanging on to this best friend bullshit. After high school I realized that we went in two different directions. I've been moreso putting up with you than thinking of you as a best friend. I don't really want your fucking man. I was trying to prove something to myself, I guess. But when it comes down to it, it doesn't need to be proven. I'm better than you are. That's the bottom line."

"So you send a fucking text message? After years of someone putting their trust in you, you send a fucking *text?* You been having her man over your house, someone who you know has a baby on the way with your friend?" That was Ginger. "You's a shady ass bitch, you know that? Real fucked up in the head. What's the difference between you and my sister? Just cuz she's a stripper? Oh, wow! Stop fucking traffic! What fucking world are you living in? HELLO! BITCH you *fucking* DO HAIR!" Ginger laughed.

"Yo, Kaycee get ya' shit together. You got two fuckin' kids and ya baby daddy is dead. Bitch you scared that won't no one love you? I'm sorry but did *you* go to school? You got a degree? Not no cosmetology bullshit. I mean a *real, actual* university degree." Ginger was cracking the fuck up at Kaycee while cutting her a new asshole. "You lucky we don't drop kick yo' ass right now, bitch. You not worth it. You're the fuckin' scum of the earth. Go back in that shop, and make ya' chump change for your little scum of the earth babies. Fucking hoodrat bitch. Ya'll hoes kill me thinking you better than the next bitch when all ya'll tiny fish swimming in the same pond. Did that go over your bald ass head or what? Get the fuck outta here."

Kaycee looked flustered. I wasn't even gonna go in hard on her like that, cuz I really did feel sorry for her. Half of me could have just whooped her ass where she stood, but I figured she wasn't worth it. Ginger jumped in and took the cake already, and really there was nothing left to be said. One look at the tears building up in Kaycee's face and you could see that enough damage was done.

Then she made a mistake. She tried to get in my sister's face. I pushed her sideways before she had a good chance to rush up on Ginger. I didn't mean to push her so hard but everyone's adrenaline was already up. She tripped and caught herself on the cement wall. She looked at me, eyes full of hate. If you asked me yesterday, I would've told you that Kaycee would never have those feelings in her eyes when she looked at me. But life is funny like that, I guess.

I put out my arm to keep Ginger from jumping all over her, and she was trying so hard. I had to turn to her and give her the stern big sister look just to let her know I had this under control. I should've kept my eyes on Kaycee. She shoved me and when I turned around she shoved me again. In a split second I was fed up beyond belief. She was smack dab in the middle of calling me a simple bitch when Ginger slapped the words straight out of her mouth.

Kaycee stumbled backward and looked hurt this time. I felt so bad. I completely forgot about the way she was tryna play me and wanted to go ask if she was okay. I was so used to having that type of relationship with her and caring about her as a person. We locked stares and without words it was clear that we were giving a last goodbye to the long friendship that we had.

Quickly, Kaycee walked back into the shop. The boldness in her blood was gone. She knew what time it was.

Ginger was shaking with rage. "If that bitch woulda hit you...

oooooh. Shit let's fucking go cuz I feel like going inside and dragging her out. Tonnie let's go. If we stay here another minute she's gonna end up calling the cops."

It wasn't that I was less angry than Ginger. I was still in shock. I nodded, and led the way, walked slowly and thought about how fast that happened. Just like that, more than ten years of friendship evaporated into thin air. I guess it was better to find out how much of a snake she really was before my child was here and I fucked around and brought all her negative vibes around my baby. In that case, thank God. It's true what they say. Everything happens for a reason.

Now I had to focus on the one I couldn't drop from my life so easily.

21

Shakima's needy ass was calling again, saying she needed even more money for little man's preschool. I could've sworn the cash I gave her for last month's fee was just yesterday. I didn't say shit, cuz too much was on my mind already. It was just easier to give in and give it up.

She tried to get a few slick words in when I showed up and handed her the money through the car window, but I was ignoring her, going through the millions of hate messages that Tonnie was sending back to back. None of it fazed me, though. Not at all. She knew she was dead fucking wrong.

She was attempting to harass me about the situation with her stupid ass home girl Kaycee, but I didn't fuck that bitch. If she asked me that face to face I could easily answer her right away. She couldn't even do the same when the tables were turned. As far as I was concerned, she was just tryna stir some shit up to take the heat off her actions. I didn't respond to any of it. I'd respond whenever she was ready to come correct with the information I asked for.

I put my phone away and attempted to push that out of my mind. I had some work to flip and some time to record my artist in the studio so that's where I was going to put my focus. Some genius once said, money over bitches. Brilliant shit.

I took care of my hustle up on Northside Drive and took the back way through the AUC to get to I20. I liked taking that route. I always caught sight of at least one fine ass college bitch all dressed up and shit. They usually couldn't touch Tonnie's sexiness regardless of what they put on, but I liked to look. Some of these young broads would end up at one of these strip clubs around here soon enough and I'd receive a proper introduction then.

By the time I got to the studio, Kaycee was blowing me up with an assload of texts, too. I didn't even waste my time reading those. I erased them right away. I wasn't in the mood for her desperate shit. The way she sold out Tonnie was so obvious and pathetic it completely turned me off of her. Not that I was really on her in the first place.

I usually used the studio as a place to zone out and think about shit, but my artist didn't show up and his mixtape was almost finished. He had to go back and redo some bars on a few songs, though. The audiences he performed for throughout Atlanta weren't responding the way we wanted. He needed places to do shows and he needed to have someone put together a street team because at this rate he was gonna have a mixtape on the street and no one would give a shit.

I wanted him to try an original approach with his rap. I even told him before that he sounded too much like Future. Then he left and came back sounding like Da Baby. He had to come out with something that set him apart but this nigga acted like he was so eager to get out on the street. Yet and still I was at the studio waiting on him for an hour and a half before I decided to say fuck it and leave. A nigga like him made me not want to try at this managing shit anymore. But he was just my first artist.

I saw money in doing this, though. Even if he wasn't the artist that was going to take me to the top, I spent a lot of time learning the game and getting practice at it just from dealing with his lazy ass. All these hood ass niggas claim they rappers and wanna get deals, but a lot of them aren't ready to put in the work. Yachty, Blueface, and Kodak Black made these niggas feel like their job as rappers was to sling a little dope here, throw money in the strip club there, and then perform and record mixtapes when they felt like it. These small time niggas weren't even close to being able to afford the lifestyle they thought they would automatically get just cuz they could make cuss words rhyme in autotune. This was all that it was teaching me. I could still use this experience in the future when I'd have my own studio and several artists to make it all worth it. Then I'd be able to live like a boss with my lady and my kids. Until then I had to pay for all this fucking time my artist was wasting, so waiting around wasn't serving me right.

Thirty minutes later I was back at my place rolling up some loud, kicked back with a bowl of off-brand frosted flakes, the TV on COPS. They was kicking down doors in some cracker ass trailer park. Some white supremacist muthafuckas in Oklahoma was running a meth lab in the back of a double wide. Like no one was gonna find out about that shit. I wasn't going to knock a nigga for his hustle, no matter what his beliefs, but them country ass Nazi niggas was stupid for that shit. They deserved to get busted.

I lit my illegal contraband and took a deep first puff. Tonnie was still blowing my phone up and it was vibrating on the edge of the end table nonstop. The more I smoked, ate, and became more comfortable…I don't know why. I just started thinking about her. I was trying to hold my ground with that woman, but the fact that she was playing around while carrying my child, that shit softened me and hurt at the same time. Truthfully, I highly doubted that anyone else was the father, but I said that shit to make her as angry as she made me. She provoked me.

The thing about my relationship with Tonnie was that we had an understanding. While she worked in the club, she played the role, and I used that setting to improve my business opportunities. Niggas around these zones knew who I was. They knew that I had money and status. They knew I had shit to blow. They could see that if they did business with me, the shit was sure to line they pockets.

Fuck all the other hoes. It was only a show. She tries to act like she doesn't know that shit, but I tell her all the time. I don't take none of them money hungry sluts home. For all the money I blew, I always made back twice as much, and if she needed it for a good reason, it was hers as long as she asked.

But her on the other hand, she violated our agreement by trying to go off and get friendly with the same nigga that be up in her ass so deep in the club that even I have to remind myself that she's just working a job. I constantly have to remind myself not to spill blood right then and there. He knows who the fuck I am, especially in relation to Tonnie, and he makes a point to push me further and further every time he deals with her in front of me. Why the fuck would she think that I'd approve of her meeting with him outside the club, even if he pays her inside the club. That's what he's *supposed* to do for her time while she's working. But if she's not working, and he's willing to break her off with that much, a nigga like me can only wonder what the fuck he's trying to buy on her spare time. With that perspective, it would take a miracle to get me to apologize to her for any damn thing. What she needed to do was just be honest with me about everything and admit her fault, and maybe I'd consider taking back what I said. Until then, I wasn't going to acknowledge that stupid shit.

I was lighting my third blunt, watching Nickelodeon, when it seemed Tonnie finally stopped buzzing my phone. I picked it up for the first time in two hours. 36 unread text messages. I deleted them all. Anything she had to tell me was going to have to wait 'til we were face to face, or at least on the phone. She disrespected me in my face and I wasn't gonna accept cheap ass words to resolve the situation.

But my ass, I fucking gave in and called her. In my high, I wanted to hear her sweet ass voice. It probably wouldn't seem so sweet right now, though. I figured she was tryna act tough all of a sudden like she didn't want to talk, cuz she sent me straight to voicemail. I didn't give a fuck about that. I called her pregnant ass right back.

"What, Dash. *Now* you wanna call me?"

"You obviously dying to get a word across. 40 fucking messages an hour and shit."

"And apparently you don't know how to read now, so…."

"Stop actin', shawty. You must have something to say since you been hunting me down all fuckin' day."

"I ain't apologizing for shit if that's what you asking for. Nigga you ain't fucking dependable and I did what I felt I needed to do. It ain't got shit to do with you if I'm tryna get my paper my way. I got a real fucking job now, anyway and I start next Monday so all that extra shit you was accusing me of, miss me with that shit."

"Oh, really, Tonnie. A real job. Doing what? You at McDondalds or some shit to be stressin' my baby all damn day while a kid calls ya' momma a bitch cuz you forgot to add pickles to his burger?"

"Why the fuck would you be so negative? No, for your fucking information I'm going to be a waitress. My sister told me about the job a few days ago. I never got to tell you cuz you been acting stupid."

"So no more club? You expect me to believe that? When we had a talk right on your bed and you told me – nah, you promised a nigga – you wouldn't step in that place again. Then when is the next time I see you naked? Coming out the back with a hand full of singles."

"What the fuck ever. I needed to earn the last little bit I needed to get my car out the shop. And no I couldn't wait months to earn that last stack working in a fucking restaurant. And no I wasn't gonna wait on you to give it to me. You give me shit but it's always on your time. Never on mine. Lately, you been tryna get better, I'll give you that much, but you know damn well your fucking promises don't ever be on time."

"Tonnie, please. I know you want ya' car back. You want ya' freedom back, cool. But why the fuck you think I'm tryna keep you away from that place? Especially after you fought? While pregnant! That shit ain't right, shawd'. Ya boy is just tryna look out."

"Yeah, a boy is exactly how the fuck you was actin'. I can't believe you accused me of cheating. You know this baby is yours. I can't believe that shit came out your mouth."

I took a deep breath and rubbed a hand down my face. I barely even felt it. I wasn't in the mood to argue for real. I picked up the remote and began flipping through channels. "Look, Tonnie. You have to understand shit from my point of view. I'm not saying that was the right shit to say, but you put me there. You know how I feel about that nigga. He be up on you like he own you. For you to run to him outside the club? It makes me look bad. It makes him feel like he got an advantage over me. Don't no nigga wanna see shit go down like that with his lady."

"So now I'm your lady? Was I your lady when you was over Kaycee house touching on her? Laying with her? That's where the fuck I just can't forgive you."

If I didn't know better, it seemed like Tonnie was talking on her end while crying. It also seemed like her friend lied to her ass and made it seem worse than it ever was.

"Who told you I touched her? Slept with her where? You believe that shit? Didn't she backstab you? And you still taking every word she say?"

"I don't know, Dash. This is where you tell me the shit isn't true. Can you make it clear for me?"

"Shit, shawty. We gon' have to make this shit clear for each other. For the damn record, ya girl is a fuckin' liar. She was sending me picture messages of her titties, her ass, her panties, all that shit. I shoulda told you 'bout it, but I wasn't sure what the fuck was going on. I admit, that was my bad. I went over to her house the morning after I found you in the club. I was heated. I wasn't thinking straight. Ain't shit happen. I saw how greasy the shit was so I left and I told her to leave me the fuck alone. I told her that shit for you, bae'. I was mad at you but I still knew right from wrong. I had a chance to change my mind and I did. Is that good enough for you, shawd'?"

"Why would you even…you know, whatever. Fuck it. I'm done with that hoe. If not for this baby I thought I would be done with you too, but my feelings just ain't letting me go with that decision. You close to the edge Dash. Don't fucking push me. I'm letting you know that now. Don't fucking do it."

"You threatening me now?"

She sniffled. "Try me and see. Just try."

I laughed that off if anything. There was nothing that she could do to me. I knew it was her hormonal rage talking.

"Well, I told you how it went down on my end. That's what it is, shawty."

"You're so fucking disgusting. You considered fucking her, didn't you."

"Yeah, I did."

"Oh my God, Dash. You make me sick. I can't…You ain't fuckin' right."

"Yeah, whatever. Give it to me straight. What's up with you and Dougie. What do I need to know about?"

22

I was so excited about today that I barely slept at all last night. Instead I was up until six in the morning watching Baby Boy and paid programming on BET. Not like I was really watching it, anyway. I was just thinking about how it would be to see Drake, dvsn, PopCaan, and Jhene Aiko in concert. I would only be a spec in the crowd, but I'd never been to such a big event before, much less inside Philips Arena. I knew the place was going to be packed and live as hell. I was ready for it. For Kenny to be there with me was the icing on the cake. Actually, the real icing on the cake was that I didn't have to pay for a damn thing. So, you could say that Kenny was really the cherry on top of the icing on the cake.

Kenny called me around ten in the morning to make sure I was up. He told me to grab all my shit and just come downstairs and get in the car as is. I left my dorm in pajama pants and a purple tinkerbell cami, shameless. All smiles. He did a quick check to make sure my nails were still on point, asked me if my hair needed a touch up, and if I just needed anything in general. I immediately saw what kind of mood he was in and I was convinced the day would only get better by the second. Kenny was the fucking bomb.com.

He drove me back to his apartment and took a shower with me. He laid me down fresh and clean on his mattress, and blessed my lips with his lips until I cried. I wasn't even sure why a simple orgasm had evoked tears. I was just already on ten and overwhelmed with anticipation to the point where I wasn't even sure it was all real. Cumming in the name of Kenny caused my joy to flood over like never before.

Around 3 o' clock, after cuddling up with each other and watching Netflix movies in the nude, Kenny told me to get dressed and began doing the same. He looked fresh to death with some brand new Yeezys on his feet and brown sand-washed jeans which weren't skinnies but they didn't sag disgustingly, either. He wore a deep blue and brown v-neck with long, fitted sleeves. He didn't pick up a hat to wear today. He put a droplet of mousse between his palms and rubbed it through his thick, shiny curls. Then he sprayed some Axe. He had more expensive stuff, but I told him the Axe was my favorite. He looked great. Just to top of his look, he put on a pair of transparent brown frames. It added a touch of sophistication to his swag. He smiled through his charcoal blue eyes when he turned to me.

"What you think?"

"I think…I'm thinking I wanna take all of that back off of you. So, don't ask me cuz…damn, Kenny. Just don't ask. Shit. You look *so* good."

I'd paused to watch him get dressed and had only accomplished the placement of my bra, panties and socks. I still sat on the bed staring as he casually approached me. He rubbed his hand between my legs, against the cotton of my panties, and he breathed up against my ear. I felt the moisture of his breath on my neck as I caught his scent in my nose. I fell weak right away.

"I wanna take you out to eat and I wanna save the dessert for later. You tryna have your sweets early?"

I shivered. How did God find this guy and why was He gracious enough to send him to me? Did I really deserve him? My God.

When I didn't say anything, too wrapped up in the fantasies he created in my mind, he pulled me by the waist and planted a kiss on my lips. "Get dressed. Where do you want to eat? I was thinking somewhere light but decent. Bonefish Grill, something like that?"

"Any of the above is fine, baby. I'd feel spoiled if we pulled up to Burger King. You couldn't spoil me any much more than you already have."

He shot me a smile that said *yeah, right* and took a seat on his bed while I stepped into my outfit. I felt like he outdid me by the time I looked in the mirror to check over my crisp navy blue and gray Jordans, a simple pair of high-waist jeans with rips at the knees, and the Boho style gray crop-tank I wore had rips and shreds of material down the sides. I made sure my bra was blue just to match my shoes since it was showing, and I let my loose deep wave hair down from a jumbo satin cap and checked to see if

I needed to fix it at all. It looked a little wild, but since it fit my look, I let it stay. I sprayed some oil sheen and finger combed it through. Kenny watched with a slim smile of his own the entire time.

"And you talk about me?"

I looked myself over once more. "Kenny, please. I look regular as hell compared to you," I said while applying mocha lip gloss.

"Regular has never looked so delicious in my entire life."

I blushed to myself and fought to not look at him through the mirror. If we caught eye contact we'd never make it out the door. He walked up behind me in the mirror and put his hands around my waist, head over my shoulder.

"Here," he said while handing his iPhone. I took mental note that it was new. He used to have an X and this new one was a 13pro. "Take a picture of us. I need to IG or something. My baby is lookin' fresh, and I'm just tryna keep up."

I shook my head and almost laughed. Once we took a few shots in the mirror he grabbed his keys and I almost grabbed mine, but he knocked my hand away.

"You'll be coming back here. Believe me."

23

Dash showed up almost three hours late to take me to my rescheduled appointment. I was trying to stay calm, knowing that over the past week, I'd placed a lot of strain on the baby. But don't get it wrong. I was livid. This was just proof that there was a drain underneath all that "*I'ma do better*" shit he was talking. It was already dead and gone. I told him that this check-up was important and somehow he didn't understand that well enough to give me his priority. Lord, the sooner I could get my car back, the better.

The appointment they originally gave me was for the clinic's opening hour. They were only open until noon on Thursdays. I don't even understand how they fit me in on such short notice. When it was half past eight I called to regretfully let them know I couldn't make it. But an act of God took place, and their very last appointment also canceled, allowing me to just push my appointment down. I wasn't sure if he'd ever come in time, but I tried my luck since it was already on my side. I told them I'd be there at 11:15.

Dash pulled up at 10:50. I was already outside. I'd been sitting out on the stairs since eight in the morning. I had only gone back in the house to pee and grab a bottled water. I was so angry my stomach was turning. I couldn't even swallow small sips, so I'd sip and spit it back out over and over again just to keep my mouth wet. When he showed up, I'd gone through the whole bottle and was bouncing it on the rail to the side of me. I stood up, pulled the back of my shirt down, and then chucked the water bottle right at his car. The bottle, empty and light, bounced off the car roof and rolled down into the curb.

I pulled at the passenger door handle and it didn't budge. He turned down his blaring music and rolled the window down. He leaned down and looked at me with a cold seriousness; the eyes of mentally deranged person. I'll admit, it set me back a step. Eyes bloodshot. The inside of his car smelled like liquor and I hadn't even got inside yet.

"You fucking crazy?"

I raked my hands down my hair and stepped away feeling like the Hulk was taking over. "You CAN'T be serious!" I exclaimed. "Dash, where you been? Why you smell like a fucking bottle of Hennessey? I needed to be at the doctor three fucking hours ago! Let me in the fucking car. Are you drunk?"

The locks unclicked and I sat down inside, keeping my distance, back up against the door. Halfway because I imagined myself swinging on him, and the other half of me was grossed out by his odor.

He never answered, just pressed down on the gas and jerked us forward toward the parking lot exit. "Dash, you been drinking! It ain't even noon. Mind you there's a baby in the car."

He turned the corner too fast and almost hit a blue car pulling out of a parking space. I grabbed onto the dashboard as the car jerked to a stop. "Fuck this," I said, quickly unlocking the doors in preparation to step out. He locked them back before I could get a good grip on the door handle.

I stopped and stared at him in total shock. I hadn't seen him like this before. It was coming from nowhere. I thought we'd got over our shit over the phone the night before and everything was on the table, clean.

He ended up apologizing about the entire Kaycee fiasco and I apologized about sneaking back into Stroker's. I told him what it was between Dougie and me – absolutely nothing. He didn't push it, just asked that I leave that nigga completely alone. It was a heavy promise to uphold because I didn't fuck with Dougie as a person as much as I fucked with him for his cash. But I agreed, simply because Dash asked. *Nicely.* He didn't demand or tell me that "*I better or else*". No shit like that. So I said I'd leave it where it last was and move on, putting our child as my first interest. That's when I asked him to take me to the doctor in the morning because the baby hadn't been checked on in over two weeks and I needed to have some blood work done.

Dash rubbed his hand down his face and pushed his head back into the headrest, taking a big deep breath as the car pulled out in front of us. I didn't appreciate that he hadn't said anything to respond to me yet.

"Hello…excuse me. What is going on? You don't even know if I still have an appointment anymore."

"You wouldn't a' been outside," he cut me off, but I continued.

"You just show up on your own time *every* time. This the same shit I'm talking about. Where the fuck you been?"

This time when he exhaled, a strong whiff of dark liquor intruded my nose and I turned for the button to lower the window. That's when I saw the droplets of blood staining the bottom part of the car door near my calves. I prayed to God it was just dark ketchup.

"You had Quani in the car with you? That ketchup on the door?"

"Where's your appointment, shawd'?"

I turned to him for a better answer, just to see him nod off and catch himself before his head touched the wheel. Something about the feel of this had my spine on ice.

"Dash. Park the car."

"Ain't you late?"

"I ain't going anywhere with you all fucked up like this. We needed you today, but whatever. I'm so not surprised. What's this on your door?"

He pressed his foot on the gas again and jerked us so hard I felt my brain smack the inside of my skull. "Park where that car left!" I didn't mean to start yelling but he was scaring me. I was breathing fast and my heart was pounding. My anger jumped up another ten levels just because I'd told myself I wouldn't get worked up today and he so easily managed to take me there.

He swung into the empty space and slammed the brakes again. In just that short amount of time the world began to spin like a carousel ride. I caught my breath and sighed, relieved that he'd shifted the car into park. Then, I took notice of the splatter stains over the middle compartment right between the seats. More dark red stains running on the part of his seat that touched the cup holders. I looked up. Speckled stains on the fabric running across the ceiling of the car, as well. My head whipped to face him. He was resting his head back with his eyes closed again. Looked asleep.

"Dash? What happened in here? Please. Did something happen this morning?"

Head still back, eyes still shut, he clutched the steering wheel tight and rolled the windows up.

"Let me in ya' place for a second. I need to chill."

"Can you answer at least one of my got damn questions? Shit! What the fuck is all these stains from?"

"If I could just chill for a second I can figure some shit out and then we can get this shit right and start setting up at my momma house and I can get you out of here. I need to lay down or somethin', shaw-"

I don't know where it came from or which one of my nerves popped last, but I reached over and slapped the shit out of him. I was already on edge and he was irritating the fuck out of me. Words were running out on his alcohol breath yet he wasn't answering any of my questions. He came back to life immediately and jumped at me. I sunk down in the passenger seat, terrified. He grabbed my wrists and got in my face. I braced myself so when he shook me, my whole body knocked into the seat over and over while he shouted.

"A NIGGA HAD THE WORST FUCKIN MORNIN'. KEEP YOUR FUCKIN' HANDS OFF ME AND LET ME IN THE FUCKIN' HOUSE. DON'T DO THAT SHIT AGAIN, MAN. I SWEAR TONNIE. A NIGGA AIN'T PLAYIN' WITH YOU TODAY. SHIT WENT BAD AND I NEED A MOMENT. GIVE ME A FUCKING MOMENT OF JUST SHUTTIN' THE FUCK UP."

"Dash, let go of me!" He let go of my wrists and I let myself out of the car just in time to vomit a soup of liquefied oatmeal and bacon into the grass. Too much excitement. The baby was stressed to its limit. I went back, opened the door and removed my purse, slammed it shut, and began to power walk back toward my apartment in hopes that I'd leave his crazy ass behind. When I looked over my shoulder, he was damn near walking beside me.

"Tonnie. Tonnie, wait up. I'm sorry, aight. I'll explain. My fault, shawd'. Shit just..." He pulled his lips in tight and kept the rest of it to himself until we reached the stairs and went up into my apartment. I walked inside first and swung the door into him, dropped my purse and keys on the couch. I stomped into the kitchen and made myself an ice cup. I didn't wanna see him, smell him, nothing. I was infuriated and afraid. I thought to call my sister just to have her on standby, but I knew she had that concert to go to. I also wasn't sure what the hell kind of drama I had just let into my home. I needed to know before I invited anyone else into the middle of it.

I crunched on a few cubes and washed my mouth out into the kitchen sink, took a few deep breaths with my palms flat on the counter and squinted at him through the space in the kitchen wall. He was leaned back across the couch with his boots up in the cushion, using my purse as a pillow. It crossed my mind to heave a knife at him where he lay.

"What. The fuck. Dash, what's with all the blood in the car? Can you please tell me if you're in danger right now? Shit, if *I'm* in danger right now? What in the hell happened to you?"

He swung his fists up to his forehead and let them rest there before rolling off the couch and falling flat on his face. I shifted my stance, purely in disbelief of what I was witnessing. If he was this fucked up how in the hell did he even manage the highway to get to my house?

I went to him and nudged him with my toes. He wouldn't budge. "I cannot believe this," I mumbled to myself. My blood pressure was up too high. I decided to leave him there. I locked the door and put the chain on, closed the blinds tight, and started a hot shower. When I got out about ten minutes later, something told me to look out of my bedroom window to where he parked the car. My eyes went so wide they could've rolled out my head.

Five police cars or more surrounded his car. They had the entrance and exit to the lot blocked off, and officers were scanning the area carefully. I saw a few cops at the other building knocking on doors. My heart was suddenly beating in my mouth.

In just a towel, I scurried into the living room and bent down to tug on his arm. "Dash! *Dash!*" I did my best to call him out of his drunken sleep at my highest whisper. He began to move a little, but didn't blink awake. "Dash!" I slapped the back of his neck and his eyes shot open. I stepped away in case he jumped at me again, but after the initial shock left his eyes, he pushed himself off the carpet and sat upright.

"What?"

"Baby, there are police all around this complex. They have your car blocked off and they searching it. What did you do, baby?" I was trying to keep my composure but fear and hormones had tears flowing down my face by then.

He just sat looking between me and the front door. His pupils shifted back and forth, panicked. Still he had yet to say anything that could make this clearer for me.

"Dash, they knocking on doors. Please go in my bathroom. Please? Oh, God. Are we going down? What the fuck did you do?"

He still smelled like he could light on fire if someone set a match too close, but he seemed to be coming back to himself. "Fuck," he muttered and then held his head up with a thumb to his forehead. "Aight. Fuck, fuck. Aight…listen. If they come to the door just front for me, aight?"

"Dash, what if they stay out there all night? Or send someone to stay out there and watch this place? Can you *please* tell me why they searching? What they lookin' for?"

"Me, Tonnie. Aight?" He stood up and went into my bedroom to look through the same window. "*Shit,"* he mumbled. "They looking for me."

"Dash. What the fuck happened!" It was no time to be raising my voice, but I was about to lose my fucking mind. I didn't understand how the day had gone this bad, this fast.

"Shh!" He came to me with his palms ready to grab me up, but he sat them on my shoulders firmly. "Just be quiet. Stay naked, they less likely bust up in here if you look like you was just showering and minding ya' business. I'll tell you after they come knocking. I want you to act as normal as possible. Can you do that for me? I ain't getting locked up today, aight? I gotta find a way to get to my son, first. I'll go in, but they don't have shit on me. I know that. Just hold me down, aight shawty?"

"They don't have shit on you? What? Besides all that fuckin' blood in your car! Does this shit have anything to do with Dougie?"

"What? The fuck you worried 'bout that nigga for, man? Stop fucking shoutin', man. Please. Shit…" Dash paced back and forth and checked his pockets. Pulled out his wallet and his phone and a small ziplock filled with smaller baggies of green. From his other pocket he pulled a stack of money folded together. Just in case, shawd'. I need to put this somewhere. Where can I stash this shit?"

The more he involved me in this the more my legs became weak just to think that there was more than just my livelihood at risk. I just wanted to know what the hell he had the baby and me involved in. We had each other's eyes locked across the room, and as my chest thumped and my nostrils flared, I wondered what kind of nigga would put his pregnant girlfriend at risk of being thrown under the jail.

24

A nigga had just got in from flippin' a little dope near the AUC and was getting ready to finally lay it down when my phone went off. It was about 4:30 in the morning. I started not to answer but I saw it was young dude Jacob calling, and dealing with him always included money in it for me. I picked up knowing I'd have to give up the idea of getting comfortable for now, but a true hustler wasn't lazy.

"Yo."

"Dash, man. You good? What it does?"

"What you need?"

"Listen I got put on to some ill shit. Got offered an entrance into the sugar game. I made a sweet negotiation, bro. I'm tryna be the next nigga up, feel me? Only thing, man, I low-balled 'em much as I could but I'm still a lil short."

"The fuck that gotta do with me? Get to the point." I sighed, already knowing what he was about to ask me.

"Listen, I'm not a new head to the hustle, ya feel me? I just need to get myself off the ground and get to the real money. I'd never have to call you like this again. I stay hungry out here for opportunities. You know that, man. I always deal with you straight and I don't try to cut no corners or short change you for the product. This is just what a nigga need, ya feel me?"

"What the fuck you getting' at, nigga? Just get to it."

"I got majority of the funds I need to cop this right quick. Was just wondering if I could hold 'bout two stacks. You front me, I make the deal, and then hit you with that return plus another two gees for the inconvenience. I'ma have the money to give back, it ain't no thang. We been doing business for a while, man. If you can come through on this, I got you, man."

I ran a hand down my fresh fade and thought it over for a

second. Jacob was a real honest young nigga. I knew that already. Sometimes he was *too* honest, but the kid was trying to come up. He was loyal. He did have a point. And he also knew when to grab his nuts and speak up. I admired the balls it took him to call me man to man with a negotiation on the table.

"How long you been fuckin' with this other party? How sure are you that they got the work you want for the money they want?"

"I seen it already, homie. I damn near touched it. They got that pure. More than enough of it. I ain't try to be greedy and ask for all of it, just what I can manage, ya feel me? Something to start off with. I can work my way up the more I do business wit' em."

"So you sure? I don't play 'bout my cash, man. If they supply you with some flaw shit I'm not gonna give a fuck if it don't take off on the street like you want it to. And don't associate my name with it at all."

"Understood. So you comin' thru with that? I gotta close this deal before eight. A nigga got school," he laughed.

I stayed straight faced and took a deep breath. I was sleepy as fuck, but if I trusted him with this I could count on an easy 200% return. "All that's nice and shit my nigga, but yeah let's just meet up at the usual spot and I'll come with that. I understand your hustle, but nigga this is still a business. No games and shit, for real. I'ma need you to come up with some collateral, man. Some real shit you can't fucking live without. It ain't about trust. It's just what it is. Get me?"

"So what you sayin'?"

"The fuck I gotta repeat? I don't give away my hard earned cash unless it's to bitches in g-strings, nigga. This ain't a favor. This is going to be an exchange. It's nothing personal. You good with me, homie. This is just the business."

"Aight, man. I got you. Same place?"

"Right."

"I'm there in twenty."

I disconnected and shook my head. This drug game was a constant. A nigga was never off the clock. I only agreed because I remembered being that young nigga hungry for something decent to hustle. The more independent you were on the street, the more money a nigga could pocket to himself. I remembered that thirst to get rid of the chain of command. I worked for self most of the time as a veteran in this game, real quiet with my moves. But I had a few business partners I convened with at the studio. We would use each other to come up on similar deals, but not too often. I fucked with them on an associate level. I wasn't into having a group of niggas surrounding me, all looking to get fed. I wasn't in the game for friendships.

By the time I reached Chamblee Tucker, it was still dark out. In another hour it would've been odd to see the two of us parked at the Walgreens before it opened. We met in the same parking spaces, the furthest from the store entrance with a little cover from the road behind two city dumpsters.

I peered through my tinted passenger window to see if he was stepping out his car yet. He was, and in the brief moment before he shut his car door again, I saw another head was in there with him. I unlocked and let him in. He sat down with a grin and dug up under his hoodie. I tensed up and got ready to reach for my piece under the seat. I watched his movements closely. He was moving a little too fast.

"Chill, man. All respect." He said and lifted his zip-up jacket to show me the butt of a glock. "This is my collateral. You want it? It's all I could come up with to trade with you. This shit ain't registered to me but my prints all on this shit. You could put me in the system with this shit if I fuck you over."

I screwed my face at him. Of all things the nigga thought to enter the trade with, he chose his gun? I guess he had a point. But if I didn't have the intent to kill anyone, what the fuck would be the use?

"Think about it. I need my shit. This my only piece. I'm going unarmed into a trade. I need this shit with me. So you know I'ma be tryna put mad deals on as soon as possible to earn my shit back." He removed it from where he had it tucked, slowly, and handed it to me butt first. I was hesitant, but I accepted.

"Who's that with you? What do they know about me?"

"Oh, nah that's my cousin Keem. We doin this together. He don't know nothin' 'bout ya, man. I ain't even said ya name. We just gotta ride up to get the dope when I'm done here. I gave you my piece but I got him for protection, ya feel–,"

Knocks on the window interrupted his sentence. I didn't peep when the cousin had come around Jacob's car and approached the passenger side of my whip, but he was knockin' on the window like it was urgent.

"The fuck?" Jacob started to roll down the window before I could put the child locks on to keep him from doing it. I would've preferred him to step outside my shit and handle that. And he rolled the window down far enough for us to see and memorize each other's face. I would've also preferred to stay anonymous to a nigga I didn't know.

This was the first moment where that voice in my head was speaking to me, telling me this shit wasn't right. At that second I realized we should've been finished with the exchange by now and too much talking had already taken place. Jacob was a young one and still hadn't learned an important lesson. When you do a deal, there's not much talking necessary. Whatever you set up is already set up and you handle business according to that plan. No words had to be involved. But yes, this had already taken too long.

The second moment my inner voice was rapping to me was when I seen the look in this nigga Keem eyes. I instantly saw no honor in the dude. In only a split second I was questioning how Jacob saw fit to trust the man. Family or not, something about this nigga wasn't right. He came to my car window with no good intention. I automatically slid my fingers to trigger position on the gun in my lap. It was a small motion he could've missed, but his eyes were locked on me.

In the very next second, the nose of a pistol was pointed at me and Jacob's eyes was as round as Interstate 285. "Yo, Keem tha fuck you doin' man? The fuck is you doin? Chill!"

"Run all this shit, yar. Car, money, all this shit."

I could've laughed if I recorded this moment and watched it later. Keem was obviously one of them niggas who hit licks and didn't know how to act when placed in the middle of higher level interactions. I could've killed Jacob for bringing this country ass nigga into the middle of it. The fact that he didn't know who I was made it worse for him. He would've known better. I wasn't about to give this rookie ass kid shit.

"Jacob, shut the fuck up. Tell ya boy to do what I tell him and we out. Where the money at?"

This was not a test. This was some real street shit and it was taking place live. I lifted Jacob's glock out my lap and popped it at Keem twice. Jacob ducked and let out a shout. The gun had to have sounded right in his ear. But Keem got hit and panicked, shooting multiple bullets into the car before he fell. I made myself as small as possible, shrinking down to use Jacob's body as a shield. All this was taking place in a matter of seconds that felt like hours.

When the shooting stopped I sat up and looked over. Jacob was dead as shit in the passenger seat, head blown. Blood was pouring from his ear and down the dashboard. His eyes were lifeless and fixed on me.

"SHIT!"

These stupid young ass motherfuckers. I reached over and opened the door best I could until it hit Keem on the ground. I leaned up to see him scrambling to try and get to his feet despite the wound in his shoulder. The way he struggled I could tell he'd never felt the burn of a bullet before. I put him out with a final shot from Jacob's gun. I never meant to become a killer in this game, but this shit got too real too fast and I was moving on auto command. A quick come-up had just become a battle of survival.

"Shit, man. Fuck!" I got back in position to drive, reversed just enough to lean over and push the passenger side all the way open, then put the car in park and turned myself to kick Jacob's body outside. Before the *thump* of his limp body hit the pavement I was on my way back to 285 South. I glanced at the time. It was 5:54 AM. I turned on the overhead lights. There was blood all over my fucking seats, dashboard, window, everything.

I switched lanes to pull off on my exit home and looked down to see that I still had Jacob's piece. As I turned the curve of the ramp I rolled down my window and threw it off the side of the road.

25

I'd never stood so close to a celebrity, and watching several of them grace the stage just yards away made the night that much more surreal. The day with Kenny already had me floating on high and nothing could've been more perfect. Drake was doing a part of his set where he slowed it down from the rap hits and told the crowd it was time for the ladies. I looked over my shoulder at Kenny as he held me around the waist and he was already on the same page, coming in for a kiss. I promise the way he looked into my eyes it felt like we'd already been married with kids at home. The way that I imagine that feeling would be, anyway. I'm saying, as if we had history; a bond that stood a test of time.

We were swaying together, standing up and vibing along with the rest of the floor section audience when a flashlight blasted my peripheral vision. Kenny and I winced at the same time and I blocked the left side of my face with an open hand, thinking some obnoxious fool left their phone flashlight on and didn't realize it. Drake's voice and music was so loud the bass boomed in my sternum, so when Kenny tightened his grip on my waist it occurred to me that he'd been trying to get my attention for a few seconds. I said, "Huh?", still focused on the stage, but Kenny's response didn't follow. I finally tore my eyes away from Drake's performance of "Jungle" to see that Kenny was actually looking directly toward the source of the light, and his expression had me scared to turn my head.

The second I saw the security guards making their way down our aisle, pushing through people and trying not to trip over chairs and feet, was the same second that Kenny tugged me and started to head down the opposite direction. Of course I didn't know exactly what was happening, but even in that moment of struggling to process, I could take a wild guess. Still, denial suppressed logic and I shouted, "Kenny? What's happening?", but I didn't think he heard me. If he did, I couldn't tell. He continued to yank us past the crowded rows and into the center aisle, where he turned us away from the stage for the exit.

Unfortunately, arena security was already posted at the double-doors, and a tall guy had a radio up to his mouth and his other hand on his ear piece, tipping on his toes, eyes darting over the people in the aisles. When he saw us I knew. We were the ones they were searching for. They were in pursuit and we, well Kenny, was wanted.

Kenny slowed down and let go of my hand, bringing both of his down in front of him in fists. He turned around and looked over my head, but not at me. Not at the desperate look in my eyes searching him for the explanation he didn't have yet. He threw his hands up onto his curly head and then spun back toward the exit. Guards were now coming from all directions and the tall man reached us first. "Sir, can I see your ticket?"

"I dropped it," Kenny lied. He had digital copies on his phone. "I had a paper copy and it's gone," he said.

"Then I need to see your ID, or you gotta go."

"What's this about?" I asked, taking a brief glimpse over my shoulder. The guards who were shuffling down our aisle had officially caught up to us, blocking us from going back toward our seats.

"ID or you're out. Now," one of them shouted from behind Kenny.

"Can you just tell us what's the problem?" I asked again.

Tall man in front of us focused on a message from his earpiece and then nodded to himself. "Both of you, we're escorting you out. Follow me and don't resist."

I took a step, but Kenny didn't and the guards behind us immediately realized he wasn't moving toward the exit as they'd asked him to. He was frozen, staring at the doors with his head tilted back, as if somehow he could see through to the other side. And he was terrified. I'd never seen this look in his eyes before. I felt a lump develop in my throat but tried to breathe through it. Whatever these guys wanted, I'm sure the best thing I could possibly do was to stay composed.

"Sir, you've gotta come with us. You don't want this to escalate. Ma'am?" This was from the one female guard out of the bunch. I could hear it in her voice that she was trying to reason with us, that something she knew was bad, and I mean *really* bad. There was a tenderness in her face, almost motherly. The one standing closest to Kenny wasn't on that, though. He lifted his radio up and said, "Yeah, it's him," and then lifted a hand to the back of Kenny's shoulder, pushing him forward.

Kenny spun to his left and shook the guy off, looking like a rabid animal pinned against the wall. "Do NOT touch me! Do NOT touch me!" Kenny lashed out, pointing a finger in the man's face. People in the back floor rows were giving us more attention now than the global superstar performing on stage.

"Kenny! No, Kenny. Look, let's step outside and see what they want. Don't do this. Please." I held out an arm to keep the guard back and he eyed us down and brought the radio up to his mouth again, turning his body slightly to hide exactly what it was that he was saying.

The double-doors to the arena corridor swung open and four-or-five men in uniform came inside. They weren't arena security. It was Atlanta PD. They didn't try to explain anything; they simply came up to each one of us and turned us around, patted us down, and cuffed us.

One of them shouted, "Akendo Olewuyo, you're under arrest for two counts of conspiracy to murder, and illegal drug distribution."

My eyelids peeled back to my edges upon hearing those words and I gazed at Drake bouncing on the stage, the slow songs having come to an end, a radio hit from his latest album bringing the entire audience to their feet in a harmonious roar. I stopped trying to fight the tears as the cuffs on my wrists were pushed in tighter. From my right hand side, Kenny's voice met my ears over the music when he shouted, "You said it wrong!"

Lips trembling, I forced a grin.

26

DOONK DOONK DOONK

The police pounded at the front door. The urge couldn't have been real because I'd just peed before I got in the shower, and yet it took my all to squeeze my bladder tightly to keep from releasing a hot stream down my leg. Standing there in the living room, naked, wrapped in nothing but a towel, I closed my eyes and tried to count backwards from ten. There was no way I could answer the door and them *not* know. It was all over my face. It was streaming from my eyes. It was dripping from my nose. It was bursting from my chest. It was trembling in my thighs. It was all over me. They would *definitely* know.

Dash was making all the commotion possible in my bedroom. Sounded like he was throwing my shit around the room looking for a hiding spot. Frantic as he was back there making *all* the noise, there was zero chance this was going to go the way he'd assured me, and I knew. I knew right there he, or I, or both, were about to go down for a crime I could only speculate was the worst of the worst.

DOONK DOONK DOONK. "Atlanta PD. Open up!"

I couldn't even call his name to tell him to kill that noise and stay still. I wouldn't go back there to tell him, either. I couldn't bring myself to move either way. Dash poked his head out and mouthed, "Open the door. Tell them you don't know anything. Ay! Ay! Stop crying! Open the door and make them leave."

But wouldn't they leave on their own if I just stayed silent and let them think no one was home? I thought. My thinking was overridden by more pounds. They were clearly trying to knock it loose from its hinges. Breonna Taylor's story flashed to the forefront of my mind and I made a decision.

The second I turned my body around, it was weird and I can't fully explain it, but either I was moving in slow motion or everything around me was being sucked into a time warp. Every sound began to echo but was muffled at the same time. The loudest thing in the room was my heartbeat. My vision wasn't even right. Everything in my peripheral darkened times ten. The only things I could see clearly was the doorknob and the shadows moving to block the light in the oblong frosted window alongside the door. I didn't recall closing the space between myself and the door handle, but somehow my palm was gripping it, and I was undoing the lock with the other. I left the chain on and cracked the door enough to just see around the jam.

"Atlanta PD, ma'am would you undo the chain?"

"I'm sorry, what's going on here?"

"Ma'am we believe that you are harboring a criminal who is wanted for arrest, we have a warrant. Please open the door and step to the side."

"A warrant to come in or a warrant for an arrest? I don't understand," I said, but my voice cracked. I tried to clear my throat but I could tell in the Hispanic man's face that it was a wrap. He knew.

"There are at least three neighbors who have already confirmed. I'm not going to ask you again. This *is* the apartment and we have a warrant for the arrest of Williard DaShon Freemont. If I have to ask again we *will* bust down this door." Officer Valasco, his name pin read, leaned back just enough so I could see other officers behind him standing with their guns out and at the ready. That death-drop feeling gripped me and nausea rose to the top.

No longer able to keep up the act, I stepped back, covering my nose, knowing that snot was on its way down with the tears. Officer Velasco elbowed his way in, popping the chain block off the door. Wood splinters flew into my face. Several more officers barreled in behind him, guns up, shouting Dash's government name, demanding that he come out and show his hands. I backed up until the wall caught me, crying terribly. The hand over my mouth was not nearly enough to hold in the rough sobs jumping from my ribs. I lowered down into a squat and hunched over, not wanting to see what would happen as they dragged him out from the bedroom.

Dash struggled with them. I could hear the shuffling. I covered my ears in case a gunshot followed. Instead, the scuffle ended and the boombastic announcement of an officer stated, "Williard Freemont you're under arrest for two counts of murder in the first degree and the unlawful sales and distribution of drugs prohibited by federal law. You have the right to remain silent, anything you say can and will be used against you in the court of law. You have the right to seek counsel. If you cannot find or afford a lawyer, one may be provided to you by the state of Georgia…"

I slunked further down in a succession of *Oh God, Oh God, Oh God*'s and forgot that one of my jobs was to hold my towel from falling away from my naked skin. My hands shielded my face and I fell away from the wall onto my knees.

They brought Dash out in cuffs first, and then gloved officers followed with his wallet, keys, phone, and drugs, all bagged up in separate ziplocks. As they exited the busted door, it was clear that more officers were in my room, pulling things apart and throwing my shit around. Dash only looked at me the second before they pushed him outside and I couldn't read his expression. It was eerily blank. All I could see were the streams of tears cascading down.

An officer came back inside and towered over me, saying something like, "I need to have a word with you ma'am. Can you please cover yourself?"

I heard the words but I couldn't make my body follow the command fast enough, and impatiently he repeated himself, adding on, "If you fail to comply I will arrest you for aiding and abetting. Cover yourself, now."

I started shaking my head so feverishly it took me standing up on both feet before I could make it stop. I pulled my towel back up and over my body, twist-tying it shut under my arm. "I'm sorry, officer. I'm sorry. Look, I'm pregnant. He showed up here, I asked him to take me to an appointment, you can call the doctor's office. I had an appointment, I'm telling you, I don't know what's happening. He showed up like that. He just showed up like that," I rambled.

The officer held his hands out and pressed the air down in front of himself. "Whoa, slow down. Gimme a second," he told me, while pulling a pen and pad from his shirt pocket. "Tell me again but slow down this time.

Take a deep breath. Go over all the events from this morning. Start from when you woke up."

I nodded, but just then, two officers emerged from my bedroom, and one of them held the cash box I kept in my closet. My body leapt forward despite my better judgment and the officer right in front of me delivered a hard palm to my breastbone, forcing me back. The one who was just walking alongside the box carrier turned and drew his weapon on me like lightning.

"Ma'am!"

"That's my money! That's my money, it has nothing to do with him! It's everything I have saved to my name. What are you doing! No!"

"Ma'am I'm not going to tell you again before you're under arrest!" He gripped my shoulder and closed the space between us, preparing to put me in some type of hold. I simply dropped my weight, and now he was holding my body like Jesus draped down from the cross.

"That's everything I have to my name, oh my God! Please don't take my money, I worked for that money, it's not his! It's not his! I swear I worked for that money!" My words were practically pureed into nonsense by the time they'd proceeded to walk the box out the door.

"I'm going to have to take you in, ma'am. You're under arrest for aiding and abetting, obstruction of justice, and resisting arrest. You have the right to remain silent..."

27

The police had their vehicles lined up behind the arena. They'd patted us down again without letting us speak – much less look – at each other, confiscated our phones, my purse, and his wallet. They had Kenny shut in the back of one vehicle, and let me sit out the back of a separate one. I was still in cuffs, but at least they hadn't closed me in as if my fate were already sealed. I kept my eyes down, an occasional tear dripping into my lap. I stared at my Jordans against the concrete.

The stench of nearby dumpsters wafted over me with each passing breeze. It was taking major concentration on my part to remain calm and take deep, soothing breaths despite it. I'd even closed my eyes for a while and tried to relive earlier moments of the day, but the sight of Kenny's sweet face next to me in bed, in the shower, or in the driver's seat of his cousin's car contrasted from the his terror in the arena, and only made me break down again and again. *Keep it together. Don't look guilty. Clear your mind,* I'd say in my head, and I'd breathe the trash odor in deep, exhaling through pursed lips.

A woman cop came over to the vehicle with my satchel purse in hand and set it on the trunk. "Your phone is in your bag," she said without looking at me. She turned her back and radioed in a few codes, then finally stepped up to where I was seated, putting a hand on the open door and another on her weapon holster, as if to remind me that she was in charge and I was obviously not. I didn't like that soft threat but I tried my best to neutralize my expression.

"Listen, your boyfriend is officially under arrest. If you don't wanna go down with him I need you to be honest with me, right here, right now. He is adamant that you know nothing about this and that you guys were simply on a date. Is that true?"

"Of course, officer. He knows I'm a big Drake fan. We were on a date. Didn't see this coming." I wanted to seem more genuine but even I could hear how rehearsed I'd sounded. I swallowed hard and tried to hit a reset button in my brain.

"Ginger…how do you pronounce your last name? Melly-yoo? Is that French?" she asked, suddenly producing my driver's license from nowhere. I guess she hadn't put *all* of the contents back in my purse.

"Probably, but the 'x' isn't silent. Mellieux."

"Hm…where's your family originally from, Ginger?"

I matched her gaze and answered, "Lakeland, Florida," very flatly. I had no idea where she was headed with all this. I could see in her face that she was expecting an answer something more exotic than that. My father is a Lake Charles creole but she didn't need those details and I doubt she gave a fuck. I wanted out of this coffee shop small talk and out of these cuffs.

"Hm…you nervous?" An even weirder question, because I mean, obviously. I didn't even answer, I just looked toward the car holding Kenny. She followed my eyes and looked down to her feet with a smirk. "Okay, listen. I'm going to let you go. I can't detain you without probable cause, and we don't think you're involved here. But again, answer me honestly. Did you witness anything strange or out of the ordinary today? Did he say or do anything concerning? Did he look worried, nervous, or anxious about anything? You know, dodging any phone calls? Tense? Antsy?"

I stared at her as if her speech was unintelligible, because it was. What was she trying to get me to say? I mean, was she expecting that I'd feel any type of pressure to snitch? Just after telling me she couldn't formally arrest me?

"Ma'am. Like I told you, I didn't see any of this coming. The only thing I felt all day was excitement to see my favorite artist. It's all I was thinking about. If I'm not officially under arrest can you take these cuffs off, please? Respectfully." I closed my eyes and scolded myself for that last bit because when a black woman says *respectfully* the way I'd just said it, it didn't sound respectful at all, nor was it meant to. She definitely picked up on that. She gripped her holster tightly, squinted my way, and then broke her grimace to look back down to her shoes again, gathering herself.

"Stand up and don't make any sudden moves. We clear?"

"Yes, ma'am." I said through tight lips. I knew this bitch wanted to rough me up or worse, just because she could. An aura of premeditated violence was oozing off of her. I stood up the same moment the car holding Kenny pulled off. Tears welled in my eyes once more, but I refused to cry in front of this officer who seemed to get off immensely on the fear of those at her mercy.

She freed my hands and gave me my ID card, pulled out a notepad, and asked me for my phone number. Then, "Is the address on your license current or do you live in the area?"

"I live in the area."

"Why is your license still a Florida license?"

"I'm a student. Isn't that allowed?"

"Ginger, what's your Atlanta address?" she asked, making it a point to disregard the salt on my tongue. I gave her my address and apartment number, reluctantly of course, and she nodded through it until replacing the pad and pen in her front pocket. "You're free to go, but tomorrow morning an officer will be at your residence to take your official statement. The only reason we're not doing that now is because my supervisor is calling us away from the scene. If you fail to respond to that officer tomorrow we will create a warrant for your arrest so my advice is to be as compliant as possible."

That didn't sound right to me, but I didn't question her, figuring that she would tell me anything right now as a scare tactic. I reached my purse from the trunk of the vehicle, choosing to say nothing else to her unless she asked a direct question. She went to the driver's side after closing the back and before ducking in to sit, she looked at me over the roof of the car. "Enjoy the rest of your night."

I snarled up my lip, realizing that what I'd actually smelled the entire time was her rotten soul.

28

When that nasty officer drove off and left me in her rearview, it not only occurred to me that I'd have to look up the MARTA route to get home, but also, I didn't have my apartment key. It was on Kenny's gotdamn computer desk. I usually strived to avoid using public transportation after 10PM, but an Uber was $28 – I looked that up, too – and the last of my parents' monthly allowance was spent in preparation for the concert. It *was* very late, but MARTA was free thanks to my student pass.

It took a bus, a train, and another bus to get to my apartment complex, and after texting Tonnie back to back and even calling to no avail, my senses were tingling. I wasn't sure if the previous situation still had me on edge, but I couldn't shake thinking that something was up on her end, as well. I could have been overthinking it, though. Pregnant Tonnie slept a lot more than her usual self. And besides, she could have been busy getting ready for a night at the club. But also, she knew to regularly look out for my texts because that was my main way to communicate. Something was off.

I knocked at my door. There was no answer. I called Asia. No answer. I called Francesca. Nothing. I kept knocking. The apartment across the walkway from mine opened and an Indian-looking girl peered around her door. I'd seen her many times before. She looked annoyed. I gave a polite smile, really not giving a fuck, and turned to knock on my own door again.

"You locked out?"

"Uh…yeah. Doesn't seem like my roommates are home or they sleep…" I paused and turned to her, giving her a chance to say something aside from just watching my struggle. She had nothing so I turned my back to her again and that's when she chose to say something else in her thick Jamaican accent.

"Do you need the number to emergency maintenance?"

"I don't have $150 to pay for emergency maintenance. Thank

you." I didn't bother to look at her this time and only heard her door shut. I called both roommates again and only Francesca answered.

"Ginger? You just called?"

I found it weird for her to open with that considering she could've called me back, but didn't. As a matter of fact, she actually sounded bothered. "Fran, it's been a wild night and long story short, my key is… listen, I'm locked out. Are you home or coming back home any time soon?"

"No. I'm sorry. I left to my girlfriend's guest house for the weekend. I'm in Macon. You've tried Asia?"

I hated dumb ass questions like that. "Yeah, Fran. Thanks. Sorry."

"Goodnight," she said, almost too sing-song for it to be anything other than sarcasm. This is exactly why I never vibed with her snotty ass.

Another call to Asia went straight to voicemail and I could only imagine that she was over her boyfriend's house, too, either knocked out cold or purposely ignoring my calls. My phone had about 20% juice left, so I resigned to having to find my way to my sister's house at that hour. I texted Porsha, my best friend in the area as well, really just to see if she was awake, before trudging back down to ground level and returning to the bus stop. Only one or two more buses would likely swing by before shutting down for the night. Routes on a Thursday quit running at 1:30 AM. Some routes, even earlier than that.

Porsha was awake, and called me after I'd revealed how the night turned out leading up to my lockout. I was already on the bus by then heading over to the East side.

"Do you think Kenny, of all people, really did what they said?"

"Porsha, of course not. I haven't known him forever but still. I *know* he's not guilty." I lowered my voice although I was way at the back and the only other passenger sat right behind the driver. "Murder? C'mon now. He's been with me all day."

"Yeah, but what if it wasn't something that happened today?"

Her point was only valid if Kenny was capable of such a thing and my patience was running short by her even entertaining the thought. I didn't share this with her to have her play devil's advocate, but I wasn't surprised. Porsha was like that, always thinking about situations from every side. Reminding myself of this allowed me to push down my budding attitude and accept that she didn't mean anything by it.

"Look, aside from this whole thing, I just need you to keep everything I just said between us. I know I don't have to worry, but still. This is really serious. I don't know what's going to happen to him. There's supposed to be a cop coming to take my statement in the morning and I can't even say what time I'll be getting back there. Shit, I might as well skip classes again tomorrow, and *shit*...I have a quiz in Chem II. That bitch ass professor isn't going to give me another chance…" I was talking to myself now more than anything.

"G, calm down. I'll come get you in the morning if you need me to take you back to your place. I don't have class on Fridays until 2:30. What time will you need me?"

"I hate to say it but probably as early as possible. What if the police show up first thing?"

"Yeah, no that's what I was thinking. So what. Seven? 7:30?"

"You know what, that's too early I'll just hop back on the MARTA."

"Nah, let me help out. It's really nothing. Let's save you the stress of not knowing. Unless you catch the very first bus, who knows how long it will take you to get back there on public transportation in morning traffic. Pssh…Atlanta? Nah, I'll give you a ride."

She was right, so I just shut up. She continued. "Look, I can't even guess what's gonna happen to Kenny. It's my first time even hearing that he out here slangin' dope. I'm still tryna process that. He's such a geek. That's wild to me. But *you* are going to be just fine. You don't wanna hear it but that's what's most important. Keep your chin up. I'm sorry your night turned out so fucked up, though. That's some crazy shit."

"I know, Porsha. I never been arrested before. They had me in handcuffs! This is so insane. I don't even know if I should tell my parents about this but like, what if I'll need a lawyer or something!"

"Ha! For what? Going to a concert with your man? Ginger. Chill. You're going to be fine."

"I hope so, P. I hope so."

"Tomorrow we should go out. In the afternoon, I mean. Or

evening. We can go to the club or a bar. Oh! Rosey O's has 75 cent wings on Friday nights. No cover charge."

That was some little pub in Sandy Springs she discovered on a date with an Irish grad student at Emory U. She swore by their menu and has been trying to get me to go there with her ever since. I was getting off at my sister's stop and didn't want to be on the phone while I walked alone, looking unaware and vulnerable.

"I'll think about it, Porsha. But that does sound cool. I'm just worried sick about Kenny. I know they have his phone and it's fucking awful to not be able to check on him or know when I'll hear from him." I almost caught myself back up in tears, but shook it off so she wouldn't be able to tell. "Look, I just got off in Clarkston. I'ma holla."

"Okay. Call me if you need anything. Oh, and text me your sister's address. Don't forget. Seven thirty, cool?"

"Cool."

"Night, chick. Chin up."

"Yeah." I disconnected the call, turning the corner on Tonnie's street and cutting through the broken fence like I always did to keep from having to walk all the way around to the parking entrance. The feeling that something could be up had never left the back of my mind and I felt a little sick to think that I could be right. There was no reason I should've been right. Still, I felt an air bubble in my throat I couldn't quite swallow.

Walking up to her building confirmed my worst fears.

I slowed to a stop and just stared at the police tape shrouding her door. I could see it without even climbing the stairs. In a mad sprint I rushed up to the landing in front of her apartment and discovered that the door was broken. Although it was shut and locked, a chunk was missing at eye level, a small chunk, but just enough for me to peer into the dark, seemingly empty apartment. "Tonnie? Sis? You in there?" I waited a while and spotted no movement; heard no reply.

I whipped my phone back out, cursed at the red battery icon, and dialed Tonnie's number. Nothing. Again and again I called my sister. It kept going directly to the automated voicemail prompt. My breathing was harried as I paced back and forth, trying to determine what was actually going on. Trying to compute that a crazy event with Kenny was eclipsing an evident crime scene at my sister's apartment, same night. I had no idea where she was. A hospital? A jail?

I stiffened and felt a cold blue charge run from my head to my toes. *A morgue?*

The gassy feeling in my chest transformed into a hollowness that made me lean over and put my hands on my knees for a moment to wait out the flip-flops in my belly. No, no, no. I was taking it too far. Wasn't no way. I scrolled down my recents log, searching for my mother's name and then out of left field, it occurred to me.

Kenny was dabbling in drugs. So does…Dash. That must've been the answer. This all, in some way, somehow, had to be *him.*

29

They had me up at Dekalb County Jail in ugly, doo doo brown jail scrubs, labeling me across the back as property of the county. They'd taken my mugshot and booked me after they dressed me. They had me waiting in an ugly room where the brick walls were covered in clumpy beige paint, stained and scribbled on, paint chipped and peeling. Just dingy looking. I sat in a chair across the bolted table from another empty chair, gazing at the double-sided mirror located on the same wall as the only entrance and exit door. A plain black and white clock hung over the door. The long hand slid clockwise ominously without a ticker hand visible to record each passing second. I stared at it blankly, taking note that I'd been sitting in this room for at least fifty minutes since a cop had last come in. And that cop had offered me a bottle of water before he disappeared. I hadn't seen him since.

Beyond all, I couldn't believe that I was sitting here like this. I'd gone from worrying about missing a doctor's appointment to worrying if I'd have to deliver a newborn baby in prison. My boyfriend had put me directly in the middle of something I had zero involvement in, and to top it all with a huge hunk of shit, the police had stolen every dollar I'd saved. Around seventeen thousand dollars. Gone. That was more than just money to fix my beater. That was my bills, my food, my emergency funds, my entire livelihood. And the new job? I was supposed to be starting on Monday. I prayed that they let me go before then and didn't do anything drastic like require bail money for my release. They didn't even offer me a phone call. If they did I'd probably call my mother or Ginger, or honestly, Dougie.

Bail or not, I needed money.

The door handle turned and in walked a lady in casual clothing. Jeans and a burgundy crew-neck tee with the words "ATL Homicide" in tiny font over her heart. In her hand was a manila folder, and around her neck she wore the type of bluetooth earphones that curved over each shoulder like a backward stethoscope. She was my same complexion, small hoop earrings, her nails done in a safe, pink and white manicure. Her hair was up in an old school French roll. I hadn't seen that hairstyle in a minute. She pulled out her chair and sighed like too much of her workday was still ahead of her, flipped open the folder as she sat, and pulled a pen from behind her ear, clicking it into function all in the same movement.

"Tonya Wendy-Ann Rhodes. Correct?"

"No one calls me Tonya," I sighed. "That's my mom's name. Please call me Tonnie."

"Sure. My name is Detective Beverly. You can call me Detective Beverly." She was still reading over the file in front of her. She had yet to look at me. I waited for her to say something else. I wasn't fazed by that lil' joke, nor was I in the mood to meet her there. I crossed my arms over my tender breasts.

"So they arrested you for obstruction, resisting, and…aiding and abetting?"

I spiked an eyebrow as she demonstrated that she could read. The question felt rhetorical as shit, but she looked at me for the first time since sitting and waited on my reply. I pulled my lips in and looked at her, matching her inquiring expression. A few seconds coursed between us and she smiled to herself like *okay, I see,* thumbing through a few more pages.

"It's all bullsh…," I stopped myself from cursing. Oddly enough this woman had me feeling like I was in the presence of an auntie, awaiting a lecture. Like somehow cursing would make my punishment worse. "It's not true. I did not aid or abet, as they're saying."

"Where is the misunderstanding?" She leaned back in her seat and tumbled the pen between her fingers.

I shrugged. "I don't know. I mean, I was hysterical. I'm hormonal, I was confused, they were talking about some Dash killed somebody. It all hit me like a whirlwind. I still don't know what's really happening."

"So where does obstruction come in? Why'd they have reason to arrest you in the first place in order to claim you resisted?"

"Detective. *I don't know.* I saw them stealing my hard-earned money and broke down. I guess I wanted to stop them? If someone was taking your entire savings right from under you, would you just stand there?"

"Hm, I don't know. Why do you have your life's savings stored in cash? Direct deposit doesn't work for you?"

"No. Actually, I'd have to have a bank account for that to work. I don't have one."

"Well, that's interesting. Why not?"

"I mean, I've got one out there somewhere with Chase but it's so far in the negative I just abandoned it. That was probably like, I don't know. Three years ago." It occurred to me that I was speaking with this woman very freely. But two things. Talking to her didn't feel like the interrogation that I kinda knew it was supposed to be, and second, I wasn't guilty of anything and I needed her to understand my position so I could get the hell up out of there.

"What do you do for a living, Ms. Rhodes?"

"I dance."

"Professional ballet?" She smirked. She knew damn well. I tilted my head and shot her a look that cussed her ass just so I wouldn't have to with my mouth. She continued to chuckle under her breath and closed the folder.

"Okay. Look. You tell me exactly how your day went starting from yesterday morning. Go slowly. I'm going to write everything down. We're both going to sign it, and then you can go."

"Really? I can go?"

"Aht aht. *After* we go over everything. From yesterday until the police knocked on your door. You got me? Not a detail missing. Can you do that?"

"Uh…yeah." I was beginning to see a light at the end of this tunnel.

"Now, seeing as I have all evening, we may need to review it a few times when we're done. I like to set appropriate expectations from the start. So if you miss a detail or change the story on me miss Tonya – Tonnie, I apologize. Tonnie, if I get the smallest idea that you're not telling me the whole truth, we will start over, and over, and over again. I got plenty of paper, plenty of pens, plenty of time. You understand me?"

I kept my eyes trained on the table between us and nodded. She didn't budge or continue to speak. When I met her at eye level she was waiting. Nothing about her face was hostile, but she damn sure looked like she was not about to play games with me. I knew what she was waiting for. I swallowed and humbled myself.

"Yes, ma'am."

Detective Beverly reanimated like we'd just set a lunch date and opened the folder again. "Perfect. Any questions before we begin?"

"Ma'am, is there a bathroom I could use?"

She grinned. "How many months are you?"

"Two."

"Well you should be at home taking it easy, shouldn't you?" She pushed back from the table. "C'mon, baby. Follow me."

I didn't expect to take a liking to Detective Beverly. I didn't want to, either. But I couldn't help it. I sort of felt like I could trust her.

30

Porsha made good on her promise several hours earlier than we'd arranged. She came through, picked me up from Tonnie's complex, and brought me to her place. The only problem was that my phone had died while I was on the phone with my mother, and Porsha had an Android, so there was no way for me to charge my phone. It was too late for her to bother her roommate for a charger.

My mother's number has stayed the same for as long as I could remember so I was able to call her back from Porsha's phone and continue spilling everything I knew about Tonnie's situation and disappearance. It was pretty cringeworthy to discover that my mother had no knowledge of Tonnie's pregnancy before this phone call, and I felt incredibly bad for stealing my sister's moment, but I had to think about that later. When it came to my description of the chain of events leading up to my discovery of Tonnie's broken door, I simply told my mother that I'd dropped my keys at the concert and every detail following the moment I arrived at my apartment remained true to life. I left Kenny's debacle completely out of it. I knew it wasn't the time to be making up stories, but it would leave my mother with more questions than answers, and let's face it. Tonnie was the one we really needed to worry about.

It was about two-thirty in the morning when I finally hung up with my mom, and as we were hanging up, she was starting her car to head up to Georgia. My dad was a night-nurse at a hospice center, and she told me she'd have him call when he got off work. I wouldn't be surprised if he showed up too, still dressed in scrubs.

Tonnie never shared the same closeness with Dad that I had, but I knew in his heart of hearts that Tonnie was just as much of his daughter as I was, and I couldn't see him reacting any differently to this than he would if it were me. If it were me, Dad would be leaving work early, actually, and probably wouldn't even stop at the house first before jumping on the highway.

I wanted to try Tonnie's line again but unfortunately it had been too long since I looked at her actual number, and she hadn't had this one that long. She changed her number at the start of the year due to an obsessed patron who harassed her outside of club hours. Porsha was sound asleep despite me running my mouth on her phone, and once I was all done it still took me an hour to close my eyes and keep them that way.

I kept picturing Tonnie in a hospital bed. Sometimes the image included hospital monitors and breathing machines, sometimes the sheets were pulled all the way over her face. When I tried not to think such morbid thoughts, I'd still get to wondering about Kenny. Was he in a jail cell? Was he being grilled by police? Beaten or roughed up? Was he alone? Was he – God forbid – somebody's eye candy for the night? It wasn't like he wasn't an extremely beautiful guy. It was a valid concern.

When I couldn't take it anymore, I tipped over to Porsha's TV stand and grabbed her silver weed pen. I took a long drag and halted at the sensations of my breath being stolen away and my chest burning. I've never favored vaping because of it. Still, I dealt with the pain and hit it again. I needed something to slow down my thoughts, or else I'd never climb out of the rabbit hole.

Porsha had me back at my apartment by 8:15 AM. I already knew Asia was back since we'd passed her car parked in the lot. When I knocked, there was still no answer, so I called her and instructed her to let me in. She looked like she'd sleepwalked to the door and didn't say a word before turning back for her room. I let her be.

I'd just plugged my phone up in my room when I heard knocking at the front door. My bedroom window didn't face the parking lot, so I couldn't be sure, but it was probably the police. I took hesitant steps, trying to mentally prepare, but one look through the peephole and the tension melted away.

"Hey mom." She came in and stepped aside for someone coming in behind her.

"I told your father what was going on and he had me pull over at a rest stop and wait for him to catch up. He's still in his work clothes. Baby-man didn't even pack a bag."

Baby-man was a strange pet-name but she'd always called him that. I rarely ever heard her refer to him by Reggie or Reginald, his actual name. Dad ducked down to come into my apartment, something he had to do to enter most doors, actually. I'd imagine Baby-man was especially awkward to someone hearing it for the first time considering he was literally 6'6". I suppose only my mother would ever get away with it.

"They don't have many visitor's spots here, do they? It's a set up," he assured me. He looked around the place and pushed his chin toward Fran's door. "That your room? Which one is it?"

"No. I have the one back there with the shared bathroom," I stated, beginning to walk toward it. My mother was pacing in the living room like she wanted to go back outside and investigate. There was no notion of needing rest in her eyes. I felt that.

"Okay, so it's legal to use this bathroom in this hall?" Dad was asking. He was being aloof on purpose and knowing him, he was only mentioning everything else than his reason for being there because he usually played the cool and collected one when Mom was having her fits. She was the panicker. The worrier. Dad had a saying: *We can't both go gray at the same time.*

I showed Dad to the bathroom and slid into my room to check my phone. Surely, it had booted up and to my delight, I'd had several missed Facetime calls and text messages from Tonnie. I snatched the poorly charged phone from its cord and bolted back into the living room. "Mom! Mom Tonnie just –,"

Strong bangs on the front door cut me short, and my mother and I exchanged glances at the sound of, "ATL PD." I could tell her mind had immediately taken her to the darkest place.

Holding Tonnie's unread messages in my hand, my new worst fear had now become having my spot blown.

31

Detective Beverly drove me home in her government vehicle and handed me her card. "I hope I won't have to, but I wanna hear from you if something happens or you don't feel safe. You hear? If I don't pick up, leave me a voicemail. I'm an old timer. Text is fine too if I'm in a meeting. Or email me. Send a messenger bird. You have my information."

I nodded, "yes, ma'am."

She wasn't lying when she said she'd drill me, and drill me she did. But she wasn't aggressive. I never felt a sense that she was doing anything more than her job. I did get the feel, however, that she was one of the best detectives the department had. It seemed like she had a lot of years under her belt, but that wasn't all. Her approach resonated with me, even in just her mannerisms as an older black woman. It commanded respect, signaled authority, yet at the same time inspired warmth and an authentic care for my well-being. I couldn't say for sure that I'd have reached the same end result had I been placed with another detective.

Detective Beverly pulled off and one look at my phone screen told the time as 5:31 AM. Damn. Even after she finished reviewing my story, I still had to go to a cell and wait for them to complete out-processing. As long as it took for them to simply sign those papers I'd have thought they were chiseling their signatures into cement slabs. It literally took about as long as the interrogation had taken just to wait for them to tell me I could leave. For some reason, Detective Beverly was still around, and personally escorted me out of the jailhouse.

I knew one thing. I couldn't have taken those dooky scrubs off and shower fast enough.

I'd scrolled through some messages my sister had sent but I didn't read them all. Mom was calling me it seems from the moment they placed my phone back in my hand and each time I saw her name appear on my screen, I declined. I wasn't ready. I could apologize later. No doubt that in whatever panic Ginger was experiencing, she'd brought Mom into it. I would have done the same, so I wasn't upset. However, I'd just spent hours going over everything and I needed a shower, some food, and some rest before I could stand to answer anyone else's questions. Ultimately, that's why I didn't immediately get back to Ginger. I tried calling her just one time while following Detective Beverly to her car but it went straight to voicemail.

I tore bands of crime scene tape away from my door and let myself in. The moment I crossed the threshold, a shudder rattled my body and I took a deep breath to stabilize. Yesterday was so traumatic. Going back inside my place, I knew immediately that I'd need to make plans to move into a new space the moment I had the money to do so.

Ugh. My money.

I flicked the light on in my bedroom and lifted my eyes to the ceiling, fed the fuck up. I somehow forgot that I wouldn't be able to just come in and get cozy in my own damn bed. The police left my shit looking like a tornado hit. My mattress wasn't even on its slats; it was thrown up against my TV and had it wedged against the wall, tilted off the dresser about a foot above the floor. I knew the second I moved the mattress and dislodged the TV, it would go crashing into the tile, so the smartest thing would be to grab the 50" LED screen first before touching anything else. Only problem, that shit would require another set of hands being as heavy as it was – shoot, the mattress, too – and I was just too tired.

A hot shower and a pack of noodles later, I propped up on the sofa finally ready to unpack my texts. I thought I'd drift asleep while reading them, that's how I was feeling when I began, but when I scrolled to the top where Ginger started last night, I sat back up, unable to believe what she was telling me.

I took it all in, and once Ginger's messages turned spastic in realizing that something had happened here and I was gone, it was pretty much more and more of the same text being repeated. I hit the camera button to Facetime, but it said that she wasn't available. I tried at least three more times before saying fuck it. Seemed like her phone was off.

Mom was sending me texts now too, telling me she was on the

way to come find me, and then saying that she was waiting for my step-dad to meet her at a rest stop and that as soon as he did, they'd be here. That she was only an hour away and she was praying that I was safe, that the baby was okay – *wait a minute.*

I texted Ginger immediately in all caps. *Y TF DID U NEED TO TELL MOM ABOUT THE BABY G?! Gah damn I cant tell u shit I swea!*

I closed my eyes, tried to put myself in my sweet baby sister's shoes, and did my best to rein it back in. I followed up with another message saying: *Sorry G. Sorry. It's been crazy for u too. I didn't mean that. I just dont think im ready to face mom wit this n now that she knows...Ginger I aint sure i even want to keep it and now mom knows. I hope u see where im coming from.*

About the shit wit Kenny tho. We need to talk asap. Im at home now. Call me or come over, hopefully b4 mom n ur dad get here. This is too crazy to b coincidence. Hmu.

Ginger didn't respond as quickly as usual, or at all. Weird, considering my family was about ready to put out an all-points-bulletin on me. You'd think she'd have been blowing me up to know I was safe and sound. Mom hadn't texted me or tried to call me again, either. I fixed the couch pillow underneath my head and imagined that the parentals had probably just got into town. Maybe that's why she hadn't seen her notifications yet.

I hoped Ginger and I would be able to help each other connect these dots. She'd recently mentioned that Kenny was in the game, and now this. There was something up with this that I just wasn't seeing. Something just beyond my scope and I could not, for the life of me, make it make sense.

The last person I wanted to speak to was Dash. After what he put me through – and this has by far topped everything, by the way – I was set if I never had to talk to that nigga again. Another reason why Ginger's confession on my behalf came at the worst time possible. But all that to say, if I could speak to Dash somehow, I'd need him to be straight up and give some type of clarification. How was all of this related?

But for real, though. Fuck that nigga. I still couldn't believe that he'd brought that insanity right to my door. He couldn't have been thinking. He has no idea what risk he put me at. I was butt-naked with a gun in my face, scared for two lives, and now dead broke because of it.

I shot upright and opened my texts. I completely forgot. I pulled up Bubble's last messages, and there it was. "Yes! Let's go!" I shouted, as if watching my football team win.

I saved Dougies number in a quickness and then sent a message.

Hey Dougie, its Sunshine. What you on today?

32

The ride to Tonnie's was a quiet one. Dad drove his Buick and Mom sat in front staring through the window over a balled fist. I could hear her sniffling, and Dad reached an assuring hand over to her knee. Mom wiped her face and fixed the radio station until she found Patti. She hadn't looked at me since the officer said the word "murder" in his line of questioning. I couldn't tell where her mind was or what she was thinking.

Somebody loves you bay-bay! Whoa, whoa whuhhh...

I caught Dad's glimpse in the rearview mirror a few times, but he didn't say anything to me, either. You'd think the cops had said that I was the one connected to the double homicide or something. But honestly, I could imagine them leaving Florida thinking one thing, and then getting here to find that the gravity of the situation is so much greater than they'd imagined. It was my fault, too. When I told Mom about this all, I purposely left my part out of it, and it totally sideswiped them both. Here they were, thinking they were on a mission for just Tonnie. Yeah, that was on me.

Dad turned the radio down after we exited I-20 and said, "You remember my buddy Freddy? He used to be your principle? His son teaches over at UNF. I'm sure if I made a call we could set up a campus tour."

This was the first thing Dad said since I'd told them that Tonnie was home safe, and it spoke volumes.

"I don't want to leave Clark, Dad. I'm not going to." His suggestion upset me more than I'd initially given it credit. No one had yet to ask me my side of this and Dad was already thinking of moving me out of Atlanta?

"Your best friend is in Jacksonville. What's her name...uh, Jennifer. Isn't she out there? Would it be so bad?"

"I haven't spoken to Jennifer since prom night, Dad. Two years ago. I wouldn't consider us *best friends* anymore. I don't want to leave

Atlanta. Period."

"Well something needs to fix you. A drug dealer, Ginger? Ginger, that sounds so far from who you are I," my mother choked over a chuckle that seemed to catch her by surprise. "I don't even know who you are these days, Ginger! What am I saying?"

"Mom! Seriously? I'm the same person you think I am! You two don't get it. I don't expect you to understand. Kenny isn't like how they made it seem."

"The minute you knew he sells drugs, Ginger, you should have got your ass out of there. You should have left that boy alone. I know I've taught you better. You know you're smarter than that. You think it's fun then, but is it fun now? Do you understand the magnitude of this? Do you understand what *danger* you could be in? Your father hasn't made it clear, but he's asking you to leave Atlanta because you *are,* Ginger. You are in danger just being in this town."

"I don't believe that I am," I said. I knew that she had a valid point and I'll admit, I was disagreeing at some points just to disagree.

She scoffed, turning in her seat. Mom squinted and shook her head. "First Tonya, now you?"

My eyebrows spiked. That blew me back. Even Dad looked over after rolling to a stop at the light. "Tonya," he whispered, softly scolding my mother.

"This wicked ass city does something to people, I'm convinced," she continued. "Maybe not Jacksonville," she said, facing forward. "But I'd advise you start researching colleges elsewhere. Taking you out mid-term is drastic, and I'd hate to make that threat. Come up with a plan and your father and I will do everything we can to make sure your transfer is successful. Don't worry about the money, don't worry about tuition or moving your things. I'll give you a few weeks. Name the school, and we'll make it happen."

In the driver's seat, Dad was nodding to her every sentence. I closed my eyes and shook my head, exhaling their nonsense. There was nothing else to say right now.

Tonnie was waiting for us in the parking lot when we pulled up. I'd texted her from before we arrived to let her know that the parents were not in a good headspace. Leaning against a random red car, Tonnie put up her fingers as a fickle greeting. Dad slowed the car in front of her. Mom rolled her window down, asked where we could park, and Tonnie said, "Anywhere."

We exchanged glances briefly and I unclicked my seatbelt. "Dad, hold up." I hopped out and Tonnie and I caught each other in a strong embrace. The cobalt blue Buick rolled away and I heard Tonnie sniffle in my ear. "Stop all that, Tonnie. It's okay."

"I know," she released me and dabbed her nose with the side of an open palm. "Nah, I'm cool. I'm just glad to see you. This shit is all so mutha'fuckin' wild."

"Oh, trust me. I know. They just found out about Kenny and Mom just said some shit in the car like 'first Tonnie, now you'," I immediately regretted repeating that.

"*What?*" Tonnie stepped back and scrunched her face. "You know what…I'm not even trippin'. Who don't know that that's how she feels about me. I'm the stripper daughter that ain't amount to shit, and now she knows I'm pregnant. She won't give two shits about Kenny once she find out my baby daddy is also a dope dealer. A fuckin' vet in the game at that. And get this, I don't know what Kenny actually did, but Dash *actually* murdered two people so," Tonnie made her eyes big as she shrugged her arms up into a Kanye shrug.

I was halted. That bit of info knocked the wind out my chest. "You said, wait. Wait, wait. You say two people? Like…a double homicide?"

"Tell me about it, sis"

Dad's voice met us from over my shoulder. "Baby girl, bring it in." Tonnie sighed, stepped around me, and wrapped her arms around my father. My mother stood alongside him, sizing Tonnie up, but still stepped in and grabbed my sister. A small yip came from my mom as she finally released a torrent of tears.

"I'm so glad to see you're alright. The worst was running through my mind," she cried. I noticed how similar the Tonyas sounded when they cry-talked, something that Tonnie had been doing a lot lately.

Dad brought a hand down my mother's back and leaned in on the group hug, whispering for Mom to calm down. He rubbed her back and then looked to me. "Can we move this inside?"

The inside of Tonnie's apartment was a mess. Her bedroom was turned upside down. Dad seemed genuinely hurt to see the state of her place. Not that he was particularly a neat freak, but I'm sure he, like I, was envisioning the place being ransacked by police as they held Tonnie at gunpoint. I'd tried my best not to reimagine the scenario, but I couldn't help it. "Aw, babygirl," Dad uttered at her bedroom doorway. Without another word he stepped inside and began to move things into their proper places.

Tonnie leaned up against the front door with her hands in the pockets of her sweatpants. She and Mom were having a stare-off.

"When you were missing…you were in jail?"

"Yes," Tonnie nodded. She rolled her eyes and reset her gaze toward the kitchen.

"Why? What happened here? Both of you arrested on the same day? No, what am I missing about all this?"

I didn't mean to, but I kinda laughed and then swallowed it. Mom spun around. "No, it's not funny. You don't even have to say it. It's just, I don't think anyone can figure it out right now." I thought back to the admission that Dash had killed two people. He was definitely at the center of Kenny's involvement somehow. And I'd known. I'd guessed it; nailed that much of it right on the head.

Just then, Tonnie just about read my mind. She began to nod and pulled her lips in. "It's Dash, isn't it?" she asked me.

"Yup. I knew it." Mom's eyes bounced back and forth like a ping pong ball. "Dash? Who's that?"

"My baby daddy," Tonnie laughed, sticking her tongue out. She clapped her hands together, and her chuckles doubled her over. "Oh, my God." she fanned the tears popping up and laughed even harder. "Yoooo. What the fuck?" She closed her laughter with a sigh and shook her head at Mom. "You wouldn't get the joke."

I was confused as fuck. I didn't get the joke, either.

33

My life was the joke. It was hard for me to imagine this shit getting any worse. My baby's father was for sure heading to prison.

You know, before I found out I was pregnant, Dash threw me for a loop and I'd almost left him. I really should have.

So just over a month ago I was doing well at the club and shit was cool. This happened right after my car engine blew and I was just learning how much Dash didn't give a shit about my schedule. I didn't realize it that much or know that he was so consistently bad at it before because I was getting myself back and forth, and I didn't have to depend on him so heavily. When he first began to demonstrate how much he sucked at showing up, I was convinced that it was because he was back with his baby momma or at least sliding with the bitch. I didn't initially realize that he was just flat out bad at moving on anyone else's time but his.

Long story short, he stayed over after bringing me in from the club one night. It was clear he'd had a few extra cups of Henny at the bar, so I pretended to fall asleep next to him as he slept it off. But really, I was just waiting. When it seemed he was out cold – and I mean dead to the world, drooling and all – I used facial recognition to unlock his phone. I went straight to his texts. I found his messages with Shakima, and other than her trashing me, there wasn't much in there to be concerned about. A sad bitch gonna hate. Didn't bother me.

I scrolled and went through the unsaved numbers instead. Some were my co-workers. He didn't really keep those conversations going aside acknowledging them and lying that he'd save their numbers. Except for the ones linking him for his product. That was fine. Didn't care. I kept scrolling.

I didn't feel this motherfucker move or sit up or none of that. All I knew was that he had my neck gripped from the back and was pulling me up by my spine. His fingers pressed into the sides of my throat and my pulse throbbed in my ears.

"The FUCK is you doin', shawd'?"

"Dash! Dash, okay! Okay!"

"Nah ain't no fuckin' okay! Bitch you goin' through a nigga phone? That's what we doin' now?"

"No! No, I'm sorry!" I held both my hands up like I was being robbed and let his phone drop onto the bed. He was kneeled up behind me and jerked my neck so hard I thought he was about to throw me across the room.

"Nah fuck that. Bitch I should buss yo' fuckin' head. We going through phones now? Where yours at? Hand it over!"

"Dash, I'm sorry! That's my fault! Babe, please let me go!"

"I said get your fucking phone!"

"Dash!" I broke down crying. He jerked my neck again, and then brought a hard fist right into my temple. I screamed, and he finally released me, jumping from the bed. He darted into my bathroom and slammed the door behind himself, still cussing me and calling me all types of bitches.

"Oh my God!" I sank into my comforter holding my head, coughing. "Get out!" I screamed at the top of my lungs. "Get the fuck out!"

He swung the bathroom door open and I cowered down when he came back over, wishing that I could actually melt through the mattress and out of his way. But he only grabbed his phone, and said, "No problem, hoe. Let me get the fuck out of here before I kill yo' stupid ass." I remained balled up in the sheets until the front door slammed.

I told myself I'd never see or speak to him again, but a voice was telling me I was dead ass wrong. What else did I expect him to do? I was dumb as hell for doing that shit with him lying right there. I cried myself to sleep that night and excused him. Maybe I was just being too insecure. I had a good run through his messages after all, and the nigga wasn't up to a thing. It was my fault, I concluded. My ass should've just chilled. Out of all the dope boys in Atlanta, I'd caught myself a good one, a rich one, a *fine* one, too. I was trippin'. I wasn't 'bout to give him back to the streets, and for what? So them other hoes in the club could jump on the opportunity and then rub it in my face?

And yet, thinking back now, I wished to God that I listened to my gut and cared less about the money or the status. What the fuck did being some kind of hood-queen mean now?

My step-father finished putting all the large items in my room back where they belonged. Ginger and I were busy refilling my dresser drawers when he walked out to my living room and immediately came back to announce that he and Mom would be getting a hotel before leaving at sunrise.

Ginger and I shared looks of relief. I grinned and turned back to folding a pile of my head scarves, at a strange peace from knowing that my sister was on the hot seat along with me this time. Which is kinda fucked up cuz I wasn't *happy* that she was. But there was a kind of solidarity happening between us, and I appreciated it.

"I'm hungry," I voiced out loud, completely disregarding Reggie. "Me, too," agreed Ginger. "You and mom leaving right this second?"

"Not if you need anything else. What is it, Ginger," Reggie asked in an expectant tone.

"If I ordered a pizza could you spot me, Dad?" I sensed Reggie's hesitation. I turned and he stood there sucking the imaginary toothpick in his mouth. There was a time long ago when as long as the man was awake, there was a toothpick crooked between the corner of his lips. He didn't break that habit until Ginger was in middle school. Every now and then, when my stepfather was annoyed or trying to navigate how to word a difficult thought, the imaginary toothpick appeared and he'd chew at the corner of his mouth. This was one of those times.

"Lemme holla at you outside the door," he motioned to Ginger. Ginger gave me a look once more and shrugged, following Reggie outside. I left it alone. Just continued folding.

Right on time, another message had come in from Dougie. It was a little hard to stay in my phone texting without Ginger noticing and asking who I was talking to. Knowing her, of course she would. I could tell she had a list of questions for me, anyway, but I knew she didn't want to be in here trying to whisper details in front of our parents. Regardless, I knew this shit had to be burning her up inside. The mystery surrounding the situation was definitely weighing on my mind, too.

I don't know how exactly the streets got the word, but once word did get out I knew it was all over Atlanta, from Conyers to Dunwoody to Union City. By time I'd first hit Dougie up this morning, he'd already heard the news. I confirmed it was true, and Dougie came back saying that he'd actually known one of the victims indirectly through a "lil chick" he dealt with. He was hitting my line now to ask if he could come check on me.

I think u meant to ask if u could take me out. I need to get out this house n breathe somewhere. I wouldn't mind a good time.

If not for his confession the other night I may have felt like I was pushing the envelope a bit, but now I was pretty confident he'd move some things around on his schedule to meet me on my request. I was activating as much charm as possible knowing what it is that I was leading up to. Dougie responded right away.

I got u. What time is good?

Thinking, I needed to be sure my parents were out of the way for the night first and that Ginger and I had the time and space to go over all of this together before I could say for sure.

Ima let u kno. In the middle of somethin rite now.

Bet. He replied.

The front door opened and shut. I put my phone to the side just as Ginger poked her head in. "I'm going with Dad to pick up some food. You want anything in particular?"

"Wings. Teriyaki sauce. Or the wings from a Chinese spot. Fried hard, either way. Fries, too. Oh, and a peach tea."

"Okay, cool. He'll drop me back here when we're done and then I guess they're going to get a room somewhere closeby."

"Okay, take Mom with you."

Ginger shook her head, smiling, and disappeared.

Well, that would be kinda quick then. Since it was now about noon, I figured I could tell Dougie to come for me around 5 PM.

That works. I'ma hit ya, was his reply. Just after reading his message, a distant sneeze put me on ice. I really thought that Mom had gone with Ginger and her husband. I didn't realize she was still sitting out there in my living room.

34

Dad shut Tonnie's door and looked up to the clouds. "I don't know how else to say this, Ginger."

"To say what? You still talking about transferring me?"

He turned his back for a second, spit, and then turned my way once more, placing nervous hands into his pockets. "This is an extremely hard thing to put into words, and I don't…" he looked over his shoulder and placed a hand around my back, flipping me to walk the same direction as him. He moved us around the corner of the landing, away from Tonnie's door. "I especially don't want your mother to hear."

"What is it, Dad?" He had me whispering now.

"I think you should consider giving your sister some space."

That jarred me for a few moments. "Why? That doesn't make any sense. You and Mom are going back. She needs someone. I have to look out for her now, especially since her boyfriend's in jail. What are you saying?"

"And that's the problem. Tonnie is not a good influence on you. It shows. Actually, you love her so much that her influence is the strongest there is. And now look at you. This close," he held up his hand, his thumb and pointer a millimeter apart. "to goin' down. You're starting to follow in her footsteps. Were you trying to impress her?"

I could see what he was trying to say, but the clearer it became, the more difficult it was to process. "Dad, what…," I scoffed and took a moment to think up the words. "Are you saying that you want me to stop talking to Tonnie? Like, cut her out of my life? My sister?"

Dad was shaking his head. "Ginger. Listen to me. I didn't say cut her out of your life. I said give her space. I been watching ya'll interact. It's like watching two best friends. Always has been. Now, you know I love Tonnie as if she was my own. I dropped everything when I heard, you understand? That's why I'm standing here in Atlanta instead of sleeping-in after my night shift in Florida. But," he paused.

"But what? How could you ask me to abandon her at a time like this? Do you hear yourself? You *say* she's like a daughter, but you don't really believe that do you? Or, this is just easy for you to say because you know Tonnie's not your actual daughter and now all of a sudden she's the villain? What. Are you trying to save me? It sounds like you're picking favorites."

"You *ARE* my favorite!" He brought a frustrated hand up to his brows and held his eyes shut for a moment. He pulled his lips in and held his hand out like he was going to continue, and then replaced his hands on his eyes. "Shit, Ginger. Listen to me and let me finish this time. I didn't mean what I just said. You're really twisting my words here and I feel like what I'm getting at is important. No one said that saying this is easy. You're wrong. This is one of the most difficult conversations I've ever had. But I need you to hear me.

"I see how you are with her and it's clear that in your eyes, she can do no wrong. Now, I've been dealing with that girl right there since she had bo-bo's in her head. I know when that girl got her first period. I was there. Years before you were a thought. And I'm telling you now. She always been a hard-headed lil thing. Always. I love that girl like she's my own, but Ginger, babygirl. You're my blood and that," he stopped to swallow down the guilt in his eyes. "That adds a lil more investment to the pot. Look here, all I'm saying is you need to take some time to step back and look at the situation. I mean really look.

"I can't speak to Tonnie like this. We both know who she is. She ain't tryna hear nothing good for her. I've watched this girl turn her life, everything she had going for her, into trash. It hurts me like hell to see her like this. You ain't ever gonna have no idea how much I hate to see it. She's getting by and no one can tell her nothing, fine. But I'm not going to stand and watch her drag you down with her and not say anything, no. You understand?"

"More or less," I nodded. Because I did, but also, they didn't. They were going to see this from a place of Tonnie being the one to blame, regardless. They didn't believe when I told them that I didn't know of

Kenny's street-association until just this past week. They never met him so they could see for themselves how much he really *did* reflect the type of girl they knew me to be. They just wouldn't get the whole picture, no matter how I told the story. And there was no convincing them that truthfully, a lot of this was coincidence. I mean, it had to be. I wanted to pick Tonnie's brain and hope that we could make something else make sense between the two of our experiences, but honestly, it was looking more and more like a big ol', crazy ol', ridiculous ass coincidence.

The only times I ever witnessed Dad look this desperate was after he'd have arguments with Mom, during those times when he was ready to apologize and get on her good side again. Deep in his heart, I knew he loved Tonnie to death, but he desperately did not want to see this get any worse for me, and I could very much understand that. How else was the man supposed to feel about it?

"I'm sorry" I sighed. "It wasn't fair what I said. You're just looking out. But honestly, Dad. I cannot emphasize enough how much this was really outside of Tonnie's control. I keep telling you, there was zero suspicion that Kenny was selling drugs. If you ask Tonnie I bet she'd tell you the same thing I would. I thought I was with some square, geeky college boy. It's not Tonnie's fault." I looked directly into Dad's eyes, earnestly. "It's really not."

He took it in and nodded for a while. Then, he held out his arms. We hugged, briefly, and he kissed my forehead. It had been a while since I got a forehead pop from my old man. It relaxed my spirit in an instant. "I love you, baby girl. Just play this smart. Play it smart, alright?"

"I know. I will. Love you, too."

Dad stepped back, went in his pocket and slid a flat fold of fifty-dollar bills into mine. "That's about $300. I want you to get a new house key ASAP. And for God's sake babygirl, I want you to leave that young man alone."

Relaxed spirit, gone. I returned a stale smile, but couldn't make my lips form the promise.

35

I stood in my doorway and leaned up by the shoulder. "Bless you," I said. Mom put her phone down, giving her undivided attention the moment she saw me standing there. I thought we were going to have another awkward staring contest, but instead, she jumped right into it as if she was just waiting for me to give her an ear.

"Are you keeping the baby, Tonnie?"

"Excuse my ears?"

"I'm just trying to figure out what your plan is. If you even have one."

"I'm working it out as I go." I admitted, caught somewhere between ashamed and offended.

"Mm hmm." She twisted her lips to the side and straightened out her shirt. "We want Ginger to either come back to go to school in Florida or pick a school of her choosing but she needs to leave Atlanta. Did she tell you that we told her that?"

"No, but it sounds about right."

"Why do you think everything is a joke?"

"What? Is it not?"

"Oh, no. I don't think both my children getting arrested in the same day, both of them sleeping with criminals and one of them being pregnant by a murderer is funny. No, not at all."

"Huh…I guess you've got the whole picture figured out then. You do remember I was old enough to know shit when I seen it back when you met Reggie, right? You ever tell Ginger that her pops was in a gang? That he also did a few months for…what was it again? Stabbing a man?"

"Self-defense. That's why it was only a couple months instead of a couple years."

"Either way. Don't act like you're squeaky clean, Mom. You're old, not innocent."

"At least I never slid down a pole to make ends meet. And at least Reggie never killed a man."

I scoffed and nearly smiled. "Oh, here we are. Now we're at the meat of it. Anything else?"

"I was scared, Tonnie. When I got the call from Ginger I was driving up here in the dark, mentally preparing to have to come identify your body. Until you have that child, if you have it, you will never know that kind of fear. You don't understand a mother's love. A mother's heartbreak to see how you've chosen to live."

"Uh huh…" I crossed my arms, unwilling to interject. I'd rather just let her get it all off her chest.

"And the same way I feel about you is how I feel about Ginger. But you're your own woman now and I can't help you if you won't help yourself. I damn sure won't be able to help Ginger if she keeps trying to follow you instead of thinking for herself. Which is why I'm asking you to come back home with us and sort your life out for my grandchild, at the very least. If not, I need you to leave your sister the fuck alone. Let her focus on school. Let her keep her head down and her grades up but just leave her out of all this craziness you have going on. The day Ginger decides she also wants to dance for money, God forbid…Tonnie I would put you in the dirt, do you hear me?"

I chuckled a little, and shook my head, eyes to the ceiling. "So no matter that she's *already* her own woman – as you seem to fail to realize – you've already decided that whatever she does wrong in her life is already my fault. I'm the problem child, right? I have some magical spell I've put on Ginger and now she has no power to make her own choices. I'm somehow pulling the strings from behind the scenes? Is that right? Or, I mean, it's always been about Ginger anyway, though right? Ever since you had her and married that man I was just an extra wheel, anyway. Is that not right?"

"Tonnie, you are purposely turning this conversation into something else."

"No, let's talk about it. You didn't jump in the car and come making ultimatums when you heard what I was doing up here. Matter of fact, if I remember this right, you actually hung up the phone on me and then refused to even talk about it. You even stopped picking up the phone for what, eight months? A year? Something like that? Where was the deep concern for my future? But no, not your precious Ginger, huh?"

"That's not fair, Tonnie. You're trying to turn this."

"You know what? I, like you, am also glad that no one has to identify my body. You're right. I was also afraid for my life when the police had me in here, tearing up the place, pointing a gun at me, putting me in handcuffs, the whole time I'm pregnant and naked. You have not once asked me how it went down, if I'm even okay, or about the baby. Oh, my bad, not until just now when the first thing you have to ask me is whether I've decided to kill it. When Dad gets back, please don't let the door hit you."

I turned and slammed myself into my bedroom, fell out on the freshly made bed and began to bawl my eyes out, immediately. I hoped she could hear me. I hoped it destroyed her and brought as much pain as she'd just inflicted on me.

36

After more than an hour out and about, Dad and I returned with a variety of bags. Food from Lucky Dragon Chinese, Chick Fil-A, Zaxbys, and a single plastic bag filled with energy drinks from the QT. "Damn, I shoulda left these in the car," Dad mumbled, realizing he'd just grabbed everything up and brought it inside.

The door shut behind us. One look at Mom and we could both tell that something had gone down in our absence. She was wiping tears out of her lids and sniffling, and did not look up to greet us, or anything. She kept her focus in her lap. I spoke up before Dad did. "You okay? Mom? You alright? Where's Tonnie?"

"In her room," Mom exhaled and finally brought her chin up. "Smells good. Which one is mine?"

"The Zaxbys. I know you like their salads," Dad answered, handing over the blue and white paper bag. "I got you a cobb with blue cheese dressing."

"Perfect. Thank you." Mom received it, looked at me one more time like she knew what I was thinking, and urged me to drop it without saying a word. I turned away from them and went to Tonnie's door, knocking before turning the handle. When I looked inside, Tonnie was on the bed perfectly still, her chest rising and falling to the cadence of cotton-soft snores. I figured it was best to let her get some rest.

"She want her food?" Dad asked, rummaging through the bags for his vegetable lo mein plate.

"No, just put hers in the microwave. She's out."

I expected them to take their food to go, but instead we camped out in the living room and ate together. For a while, no one spoke in between bites. Then Dad, determined to bring about an air of normalcy, cut the silence casually on a wholly unrelated topic, contrasting from the day's drama.

"You know, Tonya. I meant to tell you when I got home from work yesterday that I heard something through the grapevine. The assistant medical director at the home just put in for retirement and guess who they're looking to promote?" He winked.

Mom brought her shoulders back and swallowed her food. "Uh oh! Go Baby-man!"

My father blushed like he was a teenaged boy just acknowledged by his crush. They were genuinely adorable sometimes. I immediately thought about Kenny. I could easily picture Kenny as my father and myself as my mother, married for 18 years, still able to give each other butterflies the same way.

But we wouldn't be that way. Not if they threw him in prison.

Without warning, plus a mouth filled with waffle fries, I busted into tears. Mom and Dad's heads swiveled to me, and Mom dropped off the couch to scoop me into a hug right away. She sat on the floor rocking me, shooshing me, and petting my head to soothe me. I couldn't really feel it through the wig that Kenny bought.

After seeing off my parents, I went back inside to find that Tonnie was in the shower. She must have heard them gathering themselves to leave and decided not to come out to give her goodbyes. I sat on her bed and stared at the wall for a while and then went through photos on my phone just because. I began reminiscing about our last good moments together. That last photo Kenny and I had taken in his mirror. A video of him rapping Drake's lyrics to me at the concert. A selfie we took just after that where Kenny kind of looked horrible, how the photo froze him mid lip-lick, but he was still cute, in a funny way. I couldn't help but smile, ear-to-ear.

I scrolled back up to before we were dressed for the show. I bit my lip and pressed play on a video I'd taken of Kenny stroking his thick, hard dick. He sent me a seductive look and then flashed his white teeth in a goofy smile. "You freaky," he grinned. "You recording me?"

"Huh?" My voice came from behind the camera, soft-pitched and aloof, as if his question had broken me out of a trance.

"You recording me?"

"No, I'm taking a picture," I lied, still speaking softly above a whisper.

"Why you doin' that when you should be sittin' on this dick? Or my face…" Kenny stuck his tongue as far out as he could and squeezed his eyes shut, flicking his tongue at an imaginary air-clit. He couldn't keep from laughing and the camera's view dropped away from him as I joined his silly ass. The video straightened out and Kenny was in focus once more, having let go of himself now, allowing it to drop from his hand and bob for a moment between his widespread thighs. He looked down at it, and then back to the camera and nodded like, *you see it, right?*

My laughter was heard again and I said, "Yeah, but pictures last longer, though."

Kenny shook his head and nudged his chin at me, saying quickly, "No. that's a lie."

"What?"

"I said, that's a lie. I last longer."

"What? Shut up, silly."

"Put the phone down and come here."

I kept the lens on him, but at the bottom of the screen my legs slide out and my feet enter the frame. At that point I lean back so he can get a full view of my naked pussy, just to tease him. I'd visibly grabbed Kenny's desire as he sucks in his lips and smirks.

"Stop playin'. Bring it over here."

"Or what?" I continue to tease.

"Do I gotta come get that?"

"Yeah."

"I do?"

"Yeah."

"You're gonna hate me if I do."

"What? Why?"

"Cuz I'ma fuck you so good, you're gonna forget who Drake is. Fuck that concert. We won't make it. I wanna taste you. All night."

"Really?"

Kenny gets up off the bed, his large and slightly curved erection swinging just like a trunk. He gets on his knees when he's closer, and pulls me to him by my legs. He drops his head down and lashes his tongue between my lips, pulling it up and sucking in my clit in a deep swoop. I bring the camera down to catch it on video, and the last thing seen before the focal point runs up the far wall to the ceiling is my hand grasping a handful of his wild, luscious curls. I gasp and moan, "Kennyyy...," before I give it up and end the recording.

I took a deep breath and squeezed my knees together tightly after re-living one – of many – amazing moments together. Facts surrounding my reality felt so out-of-place. It had to be happening in some alternate timeline. Another dimension where shit was too fucked up to be true. Watching that video brought me back to a normal expectation, one where I could just call or text him and he'd be there on his side ready to tell me about his day, asking when he could see me again. I wanted to fucking Facetime him and see his beautiful eyes. His radiant smile. It was just crazy and unreal to imagine that yesterday could have been our last time together.

Denial buried that thought. No fucking way. We'd come out of this. He was detained, not dead. I needed to keep it together. I just had to wait it out patiently but I'd hear from him again. I couldn't lose hope in the in-between.

I was watching the video a second time when Tonnie's shower stopped. Guilty, I locked my phone and dropped it in my lap, fumbling to look normal when she opened the bathroom door. It took a minute or two, but when she emerged from the bathroom she paused and looked me over. "You look weird," was all she said.

"Were you awake when they left?"

"Yep."

"Didn't wanna say bye?"

"Not in the mood, Ginger."

"No judgment, I'm just saying."

"There's nothing to say, Ginger. Nothing else, anyway. Mom really hates me, you know that?"

I brought my hands to my knees and leaned forward until Tonnie looked at me. "Mom does not hate you, Tonnie. You sound crazy.

They're only here because they heard you were in danger and didn't hesitate to show up for you, are they not?"

"Cut the shit, Ginger. Mom would be relieved the day she gets the call. Just look, no more on that. We've got other shit to talk about and I'd rather not talk about Mom and Reggie anymore. Another day."

"O...kay." I knew it wasn't in my head. Tonnie and Mom must've had a heated discussion while Dad and I were out. I didn't press into it, though. She was right. A more important conversation needed to be had, and I was ready to iron out all of the details.

37

I don't know why I expected Ginger to have more to add to the drawing board than she actually did. It kinda seemed like we'd ended right where we started. Kenny slung dope, seemed to be rolling in dough on the low, was borrowing his cousin's car a lot, and got snatched up on conspiracy charges. Held up to Dash's involvement, it really didn't bring me any closer to a conclusion.

"Tell me again," I gnawed a chicken wing down to the bone and swallowed. "What exactly did they say when they cuffed him?"

"Two counts of conspiracy to murder. As in two murdered people. That's what that would mean, right?"

"Yeah, sounds like it."

"And you said Dash showed up with blood in his car, like that's where it happened? And it happened first thing in the morning?"

"Had to. I got off the phone with him late that night before. He showed up to take me to an appointment like mid-morning. I was being interrogated and she kept asking me what I was doing around six in the morning. Kept asking if I'd heard of him around that time. It kept getting mentioned. That's an important time. 6 AM. So common sense would say that's when he shot them. Do you know what Kenny was doing or where he was at 6 AM yesterday morning?" I channeled Detective Beverly the best I could.

"Nah. I was up at six cuz I was excited about the concert but I didn't hear from him yesterday until about 10 AM. My phone rang right as I'd started to take a nap. I specifically remember it being 10:01. So I don't know what he was up to before that." Ginger tapped her pointer fingers together just in front of her nose, deep in thought. "But wait, you don't think the two of them were actually hanging together behind our backs, though, right? Like, without us knowing? That sounds ridiculous to me."

"Yeah, me too," I admitted. I sipped my tea. "Dash liked Kenny, I think, but I can't see that they were working together without us knowing or that Kenny and him were both at that scene somehow. It's not adding up, either way."

"It's not," agreed Ginger. "But I'd think you wouldn't necessarily need to be at the scene of a crime to be labeled as a conspirator."

I hadn't thought of it that way. "You're right. So what does that mean, then? What, that Kenny set it up?"

"Set up what? A murder? Like ordered a hit? Ha!" Ginger's head wiggled on her neck in disbelief. "Now *that's* far-fetched to me."

"But what else would make the police throw a charge like that at him, Ginger? Think about it. What if he had an issue with someone and asked Dash to handle it for him when you and I weren't around to pay attention. I don't know. Maybe somehow he had Dash's number, or was left in the room alone with him while you two were over here the other day. It has to be something."

My sister wasn't buying that supposition. "Kenny was way too carefree to have something like that on his mind the entire time we were out, because think about it. While we were spending the whole day together, it would have happened already. I would've noticed that something serious was on his mind. I don't think he's the psychopath type that could be out living his best life like Kenny was, meanwhile knowing he'd just placed an order to kill two people. C'mon now. The boy wears glasses to do his homework with legit duct tape holding them together in the middle. It doesn't get more textbook nerd than that."

Touche. I went for a few fries, dissatisfied with how the microwave had stiffened them, but ate them anyway. "What if Dash was out doing business as usual, and something went wrong. What if the person he was doing business with was sent out there to do normal business but because something unplanned or unexpected threw the deal off, they're thinking Kenny sent the niggas to die, when in reality, shit just went sideways and no one could've known it would."

"Meaning that Kenny sent someone to get work from Dash and it went bad?"

"Yeah. I mean, it's niggas out here, especially the low level ones, workin' in teams all the time. And Dash ain't no killer just to be killin' niggas. I told this to the detective and I'll say it again. *IF* Dash really killed someone, best believe he was just holding himself down. He been doin this too well for too long to just randomly be out there tryna rob nobody or tryna start a war. That's just not him. So it had to have been a sour deal. So put all of that together."

"Okay, so Kenny, young in the game, is working with someone else. He's planning a full day with me so he sends his business partner on a deal. Whatever happened, it went sideways. Dash felt threatened or had to make a move quick and a nigga ends up dead. Boom. Police investigate a phone or something and find out that Kenny is the source of the connect, and pin the murder on Dash, but they think that Kenny somehow designed the situation so that someone ends up dead. I'm starting to see it. Cuz if that's the case, maybe Kenny *does* suggest the connect being that he is around Dash every now and then because of me, and is familiar with Dash enough to try to send business his way."

"Or try to buy business from," I interjected. My sister's innocence concerning the dope game was admirable and her naivety was cute. "But yes. That's crazy. Feels like we're doing a better job than the fucking homicide department right now."

"I know," Ginger agreed, reaching in for some fries. She must've realized my reluctance as I ate them. I didn't object, she could take them all if she wanted. "But Tonnie, who is the second dead person in this scenario? You said low-level guys sometimes work as teams. They ever work as threesomes? Like a lil business gang?"

I laughed. "A business gang? That's two words I ain't ever heard put together like that. Nah, I mean, maybe but that just sounds weird to me. That is a good question though."

"You didn't get any names while you were being questioned last night?"

"Nope. She was good. She went over so much shit with me but she was careful not to slip any information to me that I didn't already know."

"Hmm…this is a doozy."

"A dip muh'fucking daisy doo," I added, and we laughed together just a little bit. The suspense of being so close to an answer, yet so far from the truth, stepped in and silenced us both. Ginger and I sat there with puzzled grills.

"You know another thing," Ginger finally said to break the silence.

"What's that?"

"I know why we probably put this together before the police did."

"Why is that?"

"They probably haven't realized we're sisters. Just think. They have my statement and your statement. But we have different last names. We have different state licenses and permanent addresses, and on top of that, they booked you, but they let me go. So they only have one mugshot. If they had mine there could even be the off-chance that they'd realize we kinda look similar."

"Facts. I didn't even think about that. Ginger, you're a genius. You always think of things one level deeper than everybody else."

"It just popped up in my head. Cuz if they knew we was sisters then they'd be trying to correlate Kenny to Dash the same way we are."

"Yeah, but that would make it worse for either one of them to plead their innocence, wouldn't it?"

She picked more of my fries up and chewed, thinking once more. "Nah, I think you're right about that. If they don't know that they knew of each other before this whole thing went down it would be more believable for Kenny to say he had no idea something would go bad, and Dash at this point, if our theory is correct, could plead murder in the third degree instead of them thinking first degree; that this was something pre-planned."

I was a little lost. "Girl, the only degrees I know is the muh'fuckin' weather. I have no idea what's the difference between any of that shit, but I kinda get where you coming from."

"Hmph," she gave a half-hearted smile and then dropped it. "Either way, I don't think they're as far along in the puzzle as we are. Not without that key piece. So I'd hope it stays that way. I hope neither of them are dumb enough to mention us."

"How you think they haven't already?" I had more faith in her guy than mine. Judging off of Dash's behaviors just before they found him, I couldn't exactly rely on his logic in urgent, hopeless situations. Who knew what they were telling him to try and spoof him into spilling his guts. Shit, I hoped the nigga was lawyered up by now, if anything.

"Nah, they haven't. We'd get call backs from ATL PD if and when they do. Could you imagine them realizing that that shit slid right under their nose?"

"I don't want to."

"I feel you."

Man. Ginger is so fucking smart. It's no wonder she wasn't caught up in all this bullshit to the extent that I was. I really hated that Mom and I had to have that conversation earlier, but I hoped that she knew what I knew with confidence. Ginger was way better than me in every way. Mom had absolutely nothing to worry about.

38

My sister mentioned that she was leaving to go somewhere with a client. I was thrown off by how quickly she was moving on from one thing to the next, but I assumed that as usual with her, there was a reason according to her own grand scheme. Wasn't really my business. I could tell she was being vague on purpose, so I left her space and got on the bus back to my complex. While I was on the way, I'd looked up the number to emergency maintenance and called them to help me resolve a lock-out. Turns out to be let back in *and* get a new key was $180, not $150. Dad's cash came in clutch. I was grateful.

I took a shower and changed into house clothes, and let my phone charge for a little while, finding some chocolates to snack on from the back of my mini fridge. I liked stiff candy bars, don't know why. Propped up on a pillow, eating chocolate, watching The Circle on Netflix, I began seeing the insides of my eyelids.

My phone set off under the pillow, a muffled tune ringing that I wasn't used to. Lifting up, I could see someone was attempting to vid chat on IG. I opened the app to see that the call was coming in from a blank profile icon. I was confused. My page was private and I didn't have a lot of followers. I figured it was a rando, and I let it ring through. Two seconds later, the same profile was calling. I picked up, facing the camera to the wall.

"Who's this?"

"Is this Ginger?"

The hair on my neck stood. I didn't like weird shit like this. "Who's this?"

"This is Kenny's uncle."

Skeptical, I turned the camera around and looked at the face on the other side of the call. "How did you…do I know you?"

"We've been in contact with Kenny. He told me how to reach

you." The man looked like a lighter, heavier set version of Kenny with a splotchy beard and brown eyes. His hair was up in a bun puff, shaved down on the sides, and looking more closely, I could see that his eyes were bloodshot. "Do I have the right Ginger?"

I shook out of it and apologized. "I'm sorry. I wasn't expecting a call like this. He's okay, right? Does he need me?"

"Yeah," the man coughed and looked away from the camera. I realized he was driving. "He's at Dekalb County. He can get visitors now. We're trying to get a lawyer for him and get his bail lowered. He asked to see you ASAP. We don't know how long it could be before we can get him out."

My ears were tingling and my spine was on a cold fire. It was a blessing that he was able to get through to me somehow. I was afraid to believe this conversation was actually happening. It was very much real.

"Okay, cool. What do I have to do?"

"I don't know. Just go see him, that's it."

"Are you or any of his other family coming up to see him, too?"

"Ay, it's not just about Kenny for us, alright. Just…just, go see him. Don't call me back. I don't have the answers to nothing else. Just passing a message."

His uncle hung up and I was left confused. I didn't understand what I said wrong to rile him up that way. Furthermore, I didn't understand what that comment about it not just being about Kenny meant. All I was thinking about was how my parents had already made it up, and his people didn't even live in a different state. If he was trying to get me down there to see him, I'd assume that would only come after having seen his mother or any family at all. I was just curious to know what support he'd had thus far. I didn't mean to piss anyone off.

Nonetheless, as soon as the call ended, I was on the MARTA site putting together the route to Dekalb County Jail.

39

This bitch ass public defender across the table looked me dead in my face, already talking 'bout some damn plea deal. Tellin' me to just plead guilty, like anything that came after would benefit me. We ain't get in front the judge yet to talk about a bail amount. I ain't even have my arraignment to formally hear my charges.This sack of shit cracker was already telling me to just willingly give up my freedom and confess 'cuz it would be the "easiest" thing to do. That taking this to trial on two counts of murder would go the "hard way". I wouldn't even give this nigga solid eye contact. I wasn't hearin'shit he had to say. Not like anything I had to say mattered up to this point.

"Guard," I hollered, cuttin' off this wrinkled face muh'fucka mid-sentence. "Guard, I'm done here."

"Mr. Freemont? Mr. Freemont? I was still explaining the terms of the -,"

"Eat shit, cracka' ass nigga. I want someone else."

The guard came in and stepped aside to let me out ahead of her. Shaking my head as she followed behind down the dimly lit hallway, my chest was exploding from the inside out. Wasn't no way that nigga in there was setting up to allow me a fair shot. From jump, all he wanted was less paperwork and a paycheck. None of the shit I had going on made a difference to people like that. I wasn't shit but a box to check, so it wasn't any point tryna explain or get him to see shit from my side.

The tall, uniformed white woman led me to another private visitation room. I was expecting her to take me to my cell. I peeked inside the room and there sat a middle-aged black woman in a collared tee and a bun at the top of her head. She looked up from sifting through a stack of papers and looked back down without any change of expression or show of interest. I turned to the guard and stepped back. "This where I'm supposed to be?" The guard held her hand out impatiently as if to say *go ahead, man.*

Skeptical, I took slow steps to the empty chair and pulled it back. "Mr. Williard Freemont. Known familiarly as *Dash*..." The woman lifted her chin and her eyebrows, awaiting my confirmation.

I sat and spread my feet under the table. "That's me."

"I'm Detective Beverly, ATL Homicide."

I paused and then kissed my teeth. "What do you want? I already talked to one of ya'll. Wasted so much fuckin' time already."

"That was my counterpart. I hear ya'll didn't get off on a good foot. I'm here to send his regards. He had a prior engagement. But hopefully, we'll start over on a better note." She looked relaxed and completely unfazed by my attitude.

"Well what is this? A game of good cop bad cop? I ain't got shit else to say to ya'll, man. It's all the same with ya'll anyway."

"No. Now, Mr. Freemont. I think you'll find what I have to tell you very interesting."

"Bitch fuck you and what you think."

She looked shocked and turned it into a smug smile. "I bet you and Tonnie make quite the pair."

My ears perked. "Don't talk about my girl."

She peered at me again, her eyes poking up through her eyelashes. She knew about something, or was acting like she did. Either way, that smug grin never left her face "Look, let's get down to it. Don't you have a lawyer? I can wait for them to call him or her in before I begin." She lifted her hand to beckon the guard, but turned her palm around in a 'stop' gesture when I said, ""Fuck that lawyer. I'm not letting him represent me."

She nodded to say, *your choice* and reopened the folder on the table. Scaling down the typed form at the top of the stack with a pen, she nodded and took a deep breath. "I wanted to inform you, Mr. Freemont, that the autopsy, forensic, and ballistic reports were completed by this morning. Pretty quickly, if you ask me. I can't believe how fast they did that. Anyway, it's all completed and it shows some shocking results."

"How shocking? I told ya'll exactly what happened twenty fucking times."

"Well for one, as I know you can imagine, you could be telling us anything. I've heard it all from this side of the table. Believe me. As a matter of fact, you told my partner, but you didn't tell me. Wanna run it by me again?"

"Fuck you."

She sighed and crossed her hands on the table. "Now, Williard. I might not be able to do much about the drug charges. However, as soon as I reviewed this information for the first time, I contacted the ADA and asked him to consider having your homicide charges reduced before the arraignment from two counts of first-degree murder to a single charge of manslaughter in self-defense. I also left a message with the judge's office to postpone your arraignment until the ADA confirms. I wouldn't have gone out my way to do that if I didn't have all the evidence right here," she patted the folder, "in my hands."

A few seconds passed and she held my stare, unflinching. "I think it's reasonable to ask that you start to show a little respect."

I tilted my head back and clenched my jaws. She had already done more for me than that rent-a-lawyer was willing to do. She had my attention. "What do them reports say?"

She tilted her head from side by side. "Probably the same thing you're about to tell me. Run it from the beginning," she demanded. I brought my head forward and ran my cuffed hands over my face. I exhaled, held it in, and prepared to give her the whole story one more time.

40

Dougie pulled up. I was outside already, dressed in a tight beige cami-dress and strap-up brown sandals. I had my hair back in a ponytail with a brown and beige African-print scarf wrapped up into a bow just behind swooped edges. Chocolate shades on, lip liner and gloss popping. At the *clunk* of his locks, I opened up, grabbed the handle and hoisted myself into his peanut butter seats. I brought my D&G purse up from my arm and placed it in my lap.

"Sunshine," he nodded.

"What's up, Dougie?" I smiled. He looked me up and down, and then took off his shades, continuing to eye-fuck me from behind the steering wheel. "Thanks for coming through."

"My pleasure. What you wanna do?"

"I could eat," I grinned. "I haven't been to Atlantic Station in a minute."

"Say less." He put the car in drive and we rolled off.

"You heard from ya' boy?"

"Fuck that nigga," I said, and left it at that. Dougie, one hand on the steering wheel, turned the corner and laughed. "How's the club been these past few nights? I probably missed out on some good money this weekend fuckin' round."

"I didn't go last night. You can always go tonight."

"Sundays are slow as fuck," I whined, pushing the envelope to see if he'd offer another suggestion.

"Ay…you done with that nigga? You sure about that, Sunshine?"

"Pretty fucking sure."

"Aight. Aight, cool. That's what's up." The air was still for some moments as he approached the freeway. "Would you reconsider taking me up on my offer?"

I smirked. "Already reconsidered. That nigga wasn't no good for me. You were right. I don't know, Dougie. You were absolutely right."

He looked at me, grinning as he took the ramp. "Aight, then. Is this our first date then, Sunshine?"

I beamed. "Call me Tonnie."

Dougie bought us a three hour lane at Bowlero. I wasn't big on bowling but enjoyed the option to order some wings knowing damn well that's all I ever had a taste for. During my first turn, he stood behind me and held me at the waist, giving me guidance on how to step up and throw the ball. I rolled that shit straight into the gutter and we laughed like long time friends. I didn't realize until hanging with him in the daylight how chill he really was. In the club he kept up a too-cool appearance, unlike his lil crew; them drunk niggas like Bright who stood around acting like drooling animals. There was a different vibe here. He was allowing me to see a different side of him. A boy-next-door side. I kinda couldn't believe it.

We finished up our game. He tried to let me win, I could tell, but I just sucked so bad that I lost anyway. At the shoe return counter, he pulled out a stack of hundreds, counted it over, and handed me the whole thing. "Two stacks. Put it in your bag, bae."

I took it, grinning and shaking my head. "You weren't lying."

"Don't offend me. Nah. I said I'd take care of you. See, you ain't even gotta go in and waste ya' time tonight. Besides, you deserve some time to kick back n' relax after all that shit that nigga just put you through. Yeah, you deserve that."

I shrugged and even blushed a little. He grabbed me up and scooped me in. His hands cupped around my booty. "I been waiting for this. You already know that, right?" He was whispering, looking straight into my soul. It was unnerving. I realized right then that we were now in a relationship. I freaked out a little in my head. I didn't mind keeping this up if it meant I could get my stash up with a quickness. However, there was still the issue of this belly growing by the week. Currently, I appeared as bloated as usual whenever it was that time of the month.

He squeezed my booty and leaned down, and I relaxed and gave him the kiss he wanted. I even took my phone out right after and snapped a short video to add to my Instagram story. He held his arms up on each side of my head and flashed his watch and jewelry, grilling my camera with his chin back as I rotated my phone from left to right, duck-faced. I put a filter over the video, causing little popping hearts to float up around us, and posted. Couldn't wait for the co-worker hoes to turn up after this one. Just when they probably thought a bitch was down and out.

"Whatchu' wanna do, shawty? Wanna go to get a drink?"

"Uh," I racked my mind on what to say. Dougie had bought me drinks in the club on many occasions, so I couldn't lie and tell him that I wasn't a drinker like that. Unexpectedly, a deep hate for Dash rose up and made my mind for me. I didn't want to be attached to that sorry ass nigga. I didn't want to have to deal with birthing his child and taking my kid to prison on visitations. I didn't want to go into this knowing that I'd have to do this alone. So fuck it.

"Yeah, sounds good."

"Let's roll."

We hit a pool hall back on my side of town, closer to the club than to my apartment. The atmosphere was dark and smoky, very similar to the stripclub. The farther along in the pregnancy I became, the more that cigarette smoke turned my stomach. Even worse, it was a dude posted up near the door smoking a funky ass cigar. I did my best to ignore it.

Dougie gave a wide dap to the bartender. Their palms connected in a loud *pop.* The bartender looked at me with intrigue, and one look from Dougie cut that short. He put his head down and rubbed the back of his hands off on his apron. "What you on today, man? Ya'll wanna order some food?"

"Nah we just ate man. Let me get a henny on ice and, whatchu' drinkin' on ma?"

"Ummmm…" I hesitated, spacing out on a small, melting ice chip on the counter. It looked good, too.

"Sunshine?" Dougie pinched my shoulder, gently reviving my presence. Both their eyes were on me. "I'll take a smirnoff or something like that if you got it?"

"A smirnoff?" Dougie laughed. "I thought amaretto sour was yo' go to?"

"Yeah, but it makes me a lil sleepy sometimes. I'll keep it light."

"We got hard lemonades," the bartender intervened, before dashing to the minifridge under the far end of the bar.

I thought I'd had my mind made up. I really did. But I couldn't bring myself to voluntarily get fucked up. I'd heard that doctors allowed for one glass of red wine a day. I could sit here and nurse one hard lemonade all night. Actually, I couldn't imagine sitting in this ash tray for too much longer, anyway. I began to think up an exit.

41

Kenny's eyes welled up the minute he turned the corner and saw me on the other side of the plexiglass. He sat and picked up the phone. I was already holding one on my side, trying my best not to think about if they ever cleaned the damn things. When I saw him struggling not to cry, tears sprung down my face and there was no stopping it. I wish I'd never seen him this way.

He pulled up his chair and we stared at each other's grave expressions for a moment more. Pitch black rivets framed his face, and he sniffled and cracked a forced smile. "I'm okay, babe. Don't cry. I promise you I'm fine."

"Are you, Kenny? What's happening? Me and my s…I haven't been able to figure it out."

"My uh," he scrunched his face and looked beyond me as he struggled with his composure. "My cousin got killed and uh," he braced the phone up between his ear and shoulder in order to wipe his face clean. "I put him in touch with a friend of mine and basically, they went off and did some side shit I had no idea about. Turns out, the crazy part," he smiled that smile people make when life turns out to be crazier than ever imagined. "Is that the shooter is…well, I mean yeah, it was your sis –"

"Dash." I hurriedly cut him off. It would be stupid to assume that the words spoken on this telephone were for my ears only. "I know. It was Dash."

"Yeah so….for my involvement being what it was. I'm here. And my uncle is grieving his only son. And it's my fault," Kenny's voice cracked, and his nose flared. That's what was eating him more than anything. I knew it. A realization flashed to mind.

"Your uncle? The one who reached out?"

"What he look like? I gave my mom your IG. I don't know

which uncle she gave it to. I asked her to call you but it makes sense. She doesn't want anything to do with social media. Old lady," he almost laughed, but his lips drooped down into a tremble.

"Um, the one I guess with the faded sides and he had like, a bun on top. Kinda chubby it seemed like. I don't know, he was driving."

"That sounds like my uncle Bray."

Thinking back, he did look like he'd been up for hours or perhaps crying for hours. Either one. "His son got killed?" I asked incredulously. Is that why he was so upset with me for asking about Kenny? His comment smacked me unlike it had before.

"No. My oldest uncle Akeem's son. Akeem Jr. got killed."

I held my mouth in an 'o' for a moment and thought it all over. None of that really mattered to me. Yes, it was terrible, but I was concerned for Kenny most.

He repositioned the phone and shook his head. "Babe…Ginger I'm so sorry I got you involved in this. I was too cocky. I played this all wrong."

"Kenny. Listen. I don't care about any of it. I know who you are. I know who you're not. You don't belong in here. How long until you get out?"

Kenny shrugged. "I don't know. My mother was up here for the arraignment. She's trying to put my bail together but I mean, I don't know how long it will take."

I nodded. "I'm so glad you found a way to contact me."

"I know. Me too. I was worried if you'd come. Thank you."

I was appalled and didn't do well to hide it. "Are you kidding me? You're all I've been thinking about!" A sack of sand rose in my throat, and I struggled to continue. "The way everything happened I had zero answers. I had no idea where to turn next to find you. I'm sorry for your family's loss but thank *God* your uncle reached out. Are you crazy?"

Kenny seemed put off. "Ginger, I didn't mean it like that, I just wasn't sure if…" Kenny's voice trailed away and his face broke. He looked down and brought his hand up to press the bridge of his nose.

"Kenny," I found myself sniffling, same as him. "I love you."

Kenny's eyes shot up and he fought past the lip trembles to give forth a toothy smile. "Yeah?" I'd never told him, but it couldn't be confused with anything else. I knew those words to be true, and I'd known for a while. If there wasn't a more important time for him to know it for a fact, it was right now. "I've just wanted to be here for you. I'm here and I'll be here as much as I possibly can until you're on the other side of this," I knocked on the window.

"Ginger, I love you, too. I love you." He shook his head. "I'll never love another girl like this. You're perfect. You're everything."

I was bursting. With tears, with joy, with a pain in my chest that nothing in this second could cure. I wanted nothing more than to be able to hold him and hug him; to love on him and make love to him. I could've just disintegrated into a ball of floating ashes. The angst, the frustration, the urge to destroy this barrier and grab him, was unbearable.

The corrections officer pacing the wall stopped behind Kenny, waiting to do the wrap it up gesture once he turned and looked at him. We both took a deep, lifelong breath. "If I don't call you tomorrow afternoon, that means I'm still here."

I knew what he was asking. "And I'll be right back."

"You've got class."

"I'll make the time."

He nodded. "I'm sorry, Ginger." Kenny hung up the phone and stood facing me while his wrists were re-cuffed. He blew a kiss before taking his first steps away, and I made sure to return mine while he could still see it.

42

Dougie and I arrived back to my place around the time that I'd usually be waking up from a day nap to get ready for work. I relaxed, remembering the wad of cash in my bag. He brought the car into park, and I decided that there would be no loss in letting him know about my financial reality.

"I didn't say this before, but you know. When the police tore through my place after they took Dash, they found my savings and took it in like it was contraband. I uh…I don't keep my money in a bank. I keep cash. I go to the cash advance store right down the street over there, and change my singles for the biggest bills they have, and then I stashed in inside this pink plastic tote. They took everything I had to my name."

"Damn, bae."

"Yeah. Exactly. Saying that to say thank you. You know, for looking out. It goes a long way for me."

"Why didn't you tell me that when we was on the phone? I feel like I tried you."

"What? How?"

"Just two shitty ass racks? How much did you have before the police got it?"

"It doesn't matter," I lied. It mattered. It meant everything. "Just, thank you for everything. Not just today. Everything." I searched his eyes the best I could through the sliver of street light cutting through his windshield. I had started this speech to game him and feel him out, but as the words flowed, my sincerity deepened. Dougie leaned across the console and slid a hand up my skirt. He squeezed the outer side of my thigh and started kissing my neck. I could be crazy, but the way he was handling me, I was picking up a vibe like the nigga was really in love. He'd groped me up at the club plenty of times before, but the way this nigga was looking at me, kissing my skin slow, breathing in my ear…It was a no-brainer that he was horny as hell, but it was…sensual.

Dougie left his Tahoe running. We sat making out like that for a while, about fifteen minutes, before I pulled away and politely let him know that I had to pee. It was a little embarrassing. I'd been trying not to think about it, but as he traced circles into the space between my legs through moistening panties, it became a bother I couldn't ignore.

His wet lips trailed up to my ear. Come to think of it, as much as he'd rubbed his hands all over my body in the past, today was the first time I'd let him put his mouth on any part of me. "Sunshine?" he whispered quizzically.

I closed my eyes and exhaled through my nose. I'd be lying to say I wasn't extremely aroused. "Hm?"

"I just wanna eat that pussy."

Yeah, that was it. I pulled my lips in and calmed myself before I began to breathe any deeper. I was melting in his passenger seat. I knew Dougie was into me, but honestly, I hadn't anticipated feeling *this* into Dougie. When I envisioned the day playing out, my purpose was purely to position myself in his pocket. Suddenly, I'd envisioned us in multiple positions, period.

"Park the car and come up." Swiftly, I unbuckled my seatbelt and opened my door. "Apartment 24. Second floor." I pointed to my building and he licked his lips and nodded.

I headed up ahead of him, shocked. *Wow,* I thought. *I'm really about to fuck Dougie.* I smirked to imagine how Dash would flip if he knew. My mantra of the week was now *fuck that nigga.* Dash wasn't about to see the light of day for a long, long time.

Just to match the energy he'd given, I left my lights off and lit a scented candle. On the toilet, I removed my shoes and thought about removing my panties, but pulled them back up just to give him the privilege. I put my purse up in my closet and met him at my front door just as he walked up.

Dougie brought a palm to the back of my head immediately after the door shut behind him and began to suck on my lips. I ran my hands up under his shirt as we stumbled backward and then lifted it over his head. I brought my hands back down his back. The hard butt of his piece knocked into my right hand, and by reflex, I snatched my hands back.

"Shit, ma. My bad. Hold on." He brought a hand behind his back, pulled out a pistol, and showed me that the safety was on before he dropped it onto my couch. "It stays out here. We good?"

I nodded, and we resumed right where we left off. Dougie handled me tenderly, pressing his fingers into my booty. He brought one of them around between my legs. His other hand came back up to grip my ponytail and yank my neck down, and he buried his face under my chin, licking my skin in broad strokes. "You so fuckin' fine, I swear," he mumbled. By then we'd crossed the threshold into my room and he stopped to undo his belt.

Dougie took a step toward me and his elongated shadow danced on the wall. The blueberry vanilla flame illuminated one half of his face as he kicked off his Nikes and shook his head. He took me by the hip and pulled my body up against his, and then gripped my skirt behind me, lifting the dress up my back. I helped him and he caught my face in another kiss once the stretch material disappeared. He pulled my panties aside, and dipped down to dig a finger in. My breathing skipped. Dougie dipped down again and lifted me up by the underside of my thigh. I wrapped the other around him as he brought me to the bed. I landed on my back and Dougie got on his knees alongside the frame. Dougie pulled my panties aside, and shoved the length of his tongue inside me.

My eyes rolled and my back arched. He was already way better at this than Dash. Dash spent less than ten seconds at a time down there, doing it impatiently as if it was just another thing to get out of the way before he could start getting his rocks off. Dougie's head was different. He took his time, played with it like it wasn't only for my benefit and it was equally as fun to him. I trembled out my first orgasm. He sucked the inside of each thigh when he was ready to come up and move things along.

He stood before me in boxer briefs, and to my surprise, his body was more fit than I imagined. All this time I never knew this nigga was cut the way he was. He cupped his crotch and rolled his own eyes, watching me lie there enwrapped in bliss. He shook himself out of it and pulled his lips in, sucking my juices away. Wiping a hand down his face, Dougie lowered down onto my body. He kicked off his underwear and took my nipples into his mouth, one at a time. Dougie looked up once more as if he had to verify where he was, and propped up over me. He grabbed my hand and brought it down to his dick, wrapping my fingers around it, and then pulled my hand from the bottom to the tip.

"Wow," I whispered.

He ran his tongue across his bottom lip, smirking, and moved my hand. He just wanted me to know it. To mentally prepare. I braced myself and wrapped my arms up around his neck. Dougie took his time working himself in as deep as I could stand it, and then made love to me slowly, like the night would last forever.

43

A nigga like me had eyes and ears everywhere. That's what some failed to realize.

The holding cells in Fulton County weren't set up like people would expect from watching movies. There was too many motherfuckers to shove everybody into one. This wasn't the wild west. It wasn't exactly the worst conditions either. There were about four bunk beds, and it reminded me of the times I'd spent visiting a college girl in her campus dorm back in the day. The brick walls were covered in white paint, and there was a sink with toiletries in the corner. Unlike her dorm, a steel toilet was also in there in the corner; the lingering smell of piss the most unpleasant factor.

Since I'd gone in, I'd had two cellmates who'd already been moved out, and a new one joined me the day I'd finally face the judge. I saw recognition in his face before I'd recognized him, and when he nodded his chin up and said, "What it do, Dash," I heard his voice and placed it as one of Dougie's boys. I didn't know his name, though.

"'Sup," was all I responded.

"I heard about you. I ain't think I'd see you up in here. Thought you'd be long gone by now."

"Yeah, well you know how it goes." I said, keeping it short.

"Yeah man, the streets buzzin'. I ran into ya man's Julio down at the QT, what was it? Day before yesterday?"

"Yeah?" I asked, disinterested. I wanted him to shut the fuck up already. Julio wasn't exactly my boy, either. We'd flipped work together once or twice, and then the nigga had gone around town being loud about it like we was official business partners, which is why I'd left him alone right where I found him. His mouth was too big. No room for niggas like that in my circle.

"I went to the same high school as that nigga. Right out there in

Bankhead."

"Ay, good for ya'll. But on some real shit that has nothing to do with anything. I gotta see the judge today, and I'd appreciate some silence. I'm tryna get my mind right, man." That was the nicest way I could tell the nigga to close his mouth before he provoked my temper. Today of all days, I was antsy and nervous deep down. I was hoping I wouldn't have to save face in here in front of anybody, and was already pissed that my solitude was broken on the day I needed it most. Now here comes this nigga, tryna chat it up like we was best buddies by association.

"Oh nah, I feel you on that. You got a lot going on man."

"Uh huh," I muttered. I was pacing the floor same as before they put him in here, and ol' boy finally decided to sit on the bunk. He watched me walk back and forth, and it irritated me as much as when he couldn't be quiet. I just wanted to be in my head and this nigga was making sure that I couldn't ignore him. "The fuck you staring at, boy?"

"Honestly, I just feel bad for you, man."

"I'ma be aight. The fuck you talmbout," I mumbled to myself more than anything, continuing to pace.

"But damn, bro. All this shit, and your girl, too?"

I stopped cold in my tracks. "Fuck you just said?"

Dude cracked each one of his left fingers with his thumb, likely out of habit and focused on a spot near the door. "I'm sayin' it's a lot for a nigga to take in. Respect," and then he held his fist out like a dummy, expecting me to bump his with mine. What a goofy mutha'fucka. Either he couldn't read a room or he was purposely trying to get in my head. Counting that it was the last one, I took a step back against my desire to beat this nigga face in where he sat.

"Nigga what the fuck is you on?" I huffed. I was out of patience. "Spit out whatever the fuck it is you gettin' at." I balled my fists and clenched them behind my back so that he wouldn't see them shaking.

"Oh, you don't know, bro?" He let a few seconds tick by and his shoulders dropped. "Of course you don't know."

I immediately thought the worst, like maybe Tonnie was in the hospital or maybe she was done dirty by the police after they took me out of there and no one told me. It would explain why she hadn't come up here yet to check for me. I braced myself for him to tell me the news, already knowing I wouldn't be able to handle it if Tonnie and my baby passed away.

"Julio's bitch follows ya girl on IG n' shit. She was tellin' him Sunshine and Dougie a couple now. I was joking with Dougie yesterday and the nigga look like the happiest muh'fucka in the world. Psssh." Ol boy ran a hand over his head and smiled, reliving the moment, as if thinking about Dougie's happiness warmed him up. Shit was awkward, but beyond that, I couldn't believe my ears.

"Ya'll niggas lucky as hell. I *wish* my girl was that bad."

The beast was unleashed. Within moments, guards were in the cell pulling me off the nigga, my knuckles were busted, and the white wall aside the bunks was spackled red.

44

I was pleasantly surprised. I'd only been at it a few days, but I was enjoying my new waitressing job a lot more than I thought I would. As it approached, I felt anxious and unsure that I was built for it. But now, just having a regular job, period, gave me an unexpected pep in my step.

The first day was really just a few training videos in the back to familiarize me with company policies and standards, and then I shadowed a little bit, and brought out dishes when the kitchen was in overflow. On the second day, Greggory gave me my own tables, about two in my section per hour, and it was way easier than I bargained for. Turns out that all I had to do was keep my makeup popping and smile a lot. I pulled one-fifty in tips and I remained fully dressed the entire shift! Granted, I'd served a big birthday party – a "crash course", my co-worker called it – but it was good, honest money.

Obviously, it didn't hold a candle to making over one thousand in a night, but ever since Dougie and I became a thing the previous weekend, he was finding all kinds of sweet ways to give me money. He brought me a new Celine purse the first night I got off work to congratulate me on getting through my first day, and when I opened it, there was fifteen-hundred dollars inside. Listen when I say that the reel of that reveal broke the Gram.

The third day, yesterday, he came by during my shift and had a single appetizer. When he stood to leave, I was taking an order at another table. When I returned to his empty booth, I found a $700 tip. I scooped it up into my apron pocket quickly before anyone could tell how much money he'd put down under the corner of the plate.

I didn't have to consider going to the club for days on end, which was a huge relief being that the one thing I *could* say about waiting tables, was that the running back and forth was pretty tiring. Not unbearably tiring, especially not compared to winding and grinding all night. But the bottom line is, I was too wiped to think of doing both. Not when Baby Dash kept me feeling like there was no such thing as "enough sleep".

Dougie's Tahoe was waiting for me in the dark parking lot when I got off. That Thursday was my first time helping to close the restaurant. I was used to working late hours, of course, but I had no idea the work that went into shutting down a food establishment for the night. I didn't exactly realize that I'd signed up to vacuum floors and shit like that. I felt more tired than the days I'd been getting off at 8PM.

I pulled myself up into Dougie's truck with a Chili's to-go bag. I'd just reheated my wings so that I could get right into them when I got home, no wait or hesitation. Dougie caught a whiff of my food and shook his head, laughing lightly. "Wings, again?"

"You know it." I leaned over and we pop kissed.

"You made a good night, ma?" He asked me that after every shift, seeming as proud of me as I was of myself each time I could say I was tipped well at my *job*.

"Actually, yeah. I haven't counted it yet, but including credit card tips I think I cleared two hundred tonight."

"Look at you, making bank." I rolled my eyes playfully, knowing full and well that to him, that was chump change. I don't know. It was totally as left field as the new job was refreshing, but having Dougie as a boyfriend, not just a customer, had brought me a measure of satisfaction I couldn't have anticipated from even a foot away. In just a few days' time, I felt like I was living a brand-new life. A *way* better one.The only thought that always came along and popped my bubble was my secret.

Dougie still hadn't put the car in drive. He held his head back with a silly grin and I couldn't place what he was thinking. I looked back at him, ready for whatever sweet thing it looked like he was about to say, and swooned a little. I never thought Dougie was ugly but somehow since we'd become intimate these little things about him leveled him up in my eyes. Like his dimples, they got to me in ways they never had before. He'd clearly just got a fresh tape today and his dreads retwisted, neat and clean. He had on clear wire frames that complimented his nose ring. Had him sitting there looking like a taller, filled-out Jacquees. Nah, Dougie was kinda fine, though. I guess I used to purposely ignore it so I could maintain the boundary between us.

"Bae?" He finally said. His tone switched, and I knew he was going to hit me with a question. My brows rose in anticipation as he took another forever-pause to continue. His expression changed just a little, as if what he was going to say would be embarrassing. My head dropped on my neck in wait, and I reached out and took his hand. "What's up?" I nudged.

"How far along are you?"

At his question, my breath was stolen away, and every hair on my body stood up, electrified. He had me dead to rights. I sputtered and then stopped, closed my eyes, and fought back my composure. Without opening my eyes – I couldn't look at him – I began to respond. "Dash, I mean, Dougie," Damn this nigga really slipped the rug from under my feet. I couldn't even think straight enough to get the man's name right. My face flushed. I finally looked at him, expecting him to look utterly offended. Instead, he looked like I'd hurt his feelings. "I'm sorry. I didn't mean to –,"

"Were you ever gonna tell me?"

I swallowed hard and found that I was on the brink of crying. "I wanted to. Dougie all this shit has been happening so fast. How was I supposed to say it?"

His head barely shook left to right and he shrugged. I stared at the restaurant and watched its big signage lights shut off. He finally spoke up. "I just put a few things together, bae. I was expecting you to tell me I was crazy as hell. So it's true?"

I looked into my lap and a tear slipped out. The silence in the vehicle allowed that a soft *pap* sounded as it landed on the plastic to-go bag. Dougie had never let go of my hand and rubbed a reassuring thumb over my skin. "Don't cry, mama. Don't do that. Ay," he said, softly. "It's a beautiful thing. I'm not trippin'. I can see how I came into the picture. Wasn't shit either one of us could do to expect no shit to go down like this, ma. It actually," he stopped his speech, visibly rolling back into his memory. "Now it makes sense. When I tried to get you in the club that night. You wouldn't look at me. Something was telling me you wanted to leave that nigga, man. I knew it had to be somethin'. I thought he was putting his hands on you or suhm'. Had you scared or suhm', ya dig?"

I wiped my nose clean on my sleeve and shook my head. "Dash

is…difficult, but I was trying to ride for him. He just…he put me in a fucked up position and I can't forgive him right now."

Dougie scoffed. "I feel you. That nigga was never the one for you, bae. You was a trophy to that nigga and nothing more. I be tryin' not to come off as no hatin' ass nigga but I could tell he wasn't holding you down the way he was supposed to. I could tell you was suffering with that nigga. I told you, you the baddest, thickest, prettiest muh'fucka in Atlanta."

I sniffled and smiled. "Nah, you said the club."

"I meant Atlanta." Dougie rubbed my hand and then shifted it to interlock his fingers into mine, never taking his eyes off of me. "The first time I saw you in there, shawt', I knew if I could get you, I'd treat you like royalty, the way you deserve."

"Dougie, why were you never like this in the club? In front your guys, I get it. But even in the back. That other night was the most you've ever said to me back there."

"Fuck, bae. Look at you. I ain't never been around a bitch had me as nervous as when I been around you. Never. I just wanted to snatch you up out of there and show you instead of tell you. But I had a position to play, too, feel me? All I could do is just bless you best I could." With that, he let go of my hand, lifted up, and took out another stack of money. I needed it, God knows, and all was going exceedingly well beyond my initial scheme to keep him hooked and generous. But now, as I was developing feelings – and fast – I felt the need to give him a special kind of reassurance.

He began flicking bills from one hand to the other, counting. I waved my hand up and interrupted. "Dougie."

His head snapped up and his eyes darted to mine. I rested my hand on his wrist and said, "Just so you know, I really like you. You don't have to give me money *every* time we're together. You don't have to pay me to stay with you."

His smile lingered for a while and he lowered his money-filled hands into his lap. "Sunshine. This is why you're my favorite. You pretty, but not stuck-up. You ain't greedy, either. You sweet as hell. That's why you deserve all this. It ain't breakin' my pocket, man. Trust me." He lifted his hands up, put the stack back together and prepared to start counting again. "You said all your savings got taken away so just let me make sure you straight. Aight?"

I nodded and did as I was told, adding nothing more in rebuttal. I was damn sure right about one thing. Aint no way this nigga wasn't in love with me. I wasn't at all used to a hood nigga being so open and clear about his every thought and feeling, but I could get used to it. That's a fact.

"You work tomorrow?" he asked, handing me a portion of the stack. "That's six-hundred. I gotta re-up tomorrow so I'm holding on to the rest of this," he added, giving me an explanation I didn't even need.

"I'm off. I work again Saturday," I replied, assuming he was curious to know my schedule for the purpose of picking me up and having to drop me back off.

"Even better. Be ready by 'bout 11."

"In the morning? Why?"

He sat back and replaced the rest of the cash in his pocket, then whipped his head to me and held in his lips. He reached out and pinched at my chin, "So we can go pick up your new car."

My jaw dropped to the floor.

45

Kenny's mother pulled the necessary strings to post his bail. By Thursday afternoon, he was out. By Thursday night, I was at his place. As luck should have it, we had the apartment to ourselves since his roommates, a pair of brothers, had already gone home for that weekend. His mother was staying elsewhere with a family member, and so there was no pressure and complete privacy.

Kenny and I showered together and started the love-making there. It moved from the shower to the bathroom counter, to the bedroom floor, and finally the bed. We finally fell asleep after coasting on a sex-high, but it was really more like a nap because once Kenny woke to go pee, he returned and brought me back to life with amazing head, which revved everything back up again.

Kenny blessed me with his tongue until I cried real tears. The tears wouldn't stop and the shuddering intensified until he finally scaled up my body and held me closely, forehead to forehead.

"I was so worried about you. I missed this so much." The soggy words ran from my lips in a continuous note, as I tried – and failed – to maintain my ugly-cry face. The wells of his eyes were also filled with water, and for at least an hour after he managed to calm me, we lay there, our bodies tightly woven together as if only an act of God could pry us apart. Kenny landed an occasional kiss on my forehead, and of course, it was the one thing he could do that was sure to bring my nerves down to an absolute still. Our heartbeats felt aligned, and I eased back into a happy place, completely zen, basking in his beautiful scent.

His hands rubbed up and down my back, and then up and down my booty, and then we were making out again, moaning into each other. The sex that followed took an aggressive turn, and he fucked me relentlessly, reminding me that I could scream and moan as loudly as I wanted. At one point, I was being piled off the end of the bed, holding myself up in a backbend. Literally *shouting* his name. Kenny groaned out a monstrous nut, and growled deeply from his chest as he pulled out and sprinkled warm fluid down my gooch. I relaxed and had no choice but to fall on my head and do a half-hearted tumble onto wobbly feet. "Got dammit, Kenny," I squeaked, rushing to the bathroom for a rag.

I could hear his laughter from the room, free and full. Kenny eased up behind me as I washed up at his bathroom sink and grabbed me around the waist. We looked at us in the mirror, same as we did the day we left for the concert. This time, the mood shifted, and we both held solemn stares, exchanging thoughts telepathically. Still, he had to say it.

"It isn't over, is it?" He asked, referring to the upcoming court motions and eventual trial.

I pursed my lips and closed my eyes. I didn't want to think about it, but he was right, it was kind of looming over our heads in every move we made. Kenny rubbed his hands down over my thighs and kissed my face, right by my ear. He whispered, "I love you, Ginger."

"I love you too, Kenny. So much."

It was great to finally be able to say it without an ounce of apprehension or fear, and we were saying it to each other as often as we remembered, as many times as allowed in the nooks and spaces of time between our fantastic highs. There were plenty of moments like this throughout the night when we each had to stop, acknowledge reality, and count the blessing that was us, right here, right now.

I returned to his bed and stepped over my pile of clothes on the ground, picking up my phone for the time. Only then did I remember I'd turned my phone off when we'd got here to demonstrate how much Kenny had my full attention. Subsequently, I turned my head for his Mandalorian desk clock. It was 4:42 AM. I had class and so did he. Although he was the one who'd been locked up, I knew for sure that I was going to have to bust my ass the remainder of the semester to make up for all the classes I'd been missing, too. Kenny climbed on the bed and lay back with his arms crossed over his forehead. He closed his eyes, and by the time I went to pee and return, he was snoring softly. I spread out over his chest and went where he was, joining him on a peaceful cloud.

I was well into missing my first class of the morning. Even as I'd thought about it, I didn't turn on my phone to set an alarm. Instead, we were awoken by forceful pounds on his front door. We both jumped awake, and I immediately checked the time displayed on Kenny's desk. 8:55. Kenny was rounding the bed and reaching up in his closet as I stepped into my underwear.

"Kenny! Open up! I just wanna have a word wit'cha."

Kenny paused, sliding the gun he'd produced from the top of his closet back underneath a folded stack of towels. I didn't have a moment to be unnerved by one thing at a time. Kenny stepped over to his sprawled clothing and began getting dressed, too. "What the fuck, man," he mumbled. The pounding didn't stop.

"Who's that?" I whispered. I wasn't sure if I needed to hide, go to escape through the sliding patio doors, or what. Didn't sound like the police. I figured if it was, they would've announced themselves as such by now.

Kenny sucked his teeth and pulled on his T-shirt. "Sounds like my uncle. Just stay here. Don't come out. I'm serious"

Kenny enclosed me in his bedroom and I hung around at the door frame, eavesdropping the best I could. I heard him undo the locks and the chain. "Uncle Keem?"

"Why was it my boy and not you? What made you send him instead of you? I heard it was pussy. That true?"

"Whoa, whoa. Uncle Keem. Mom know you here? You not supposed to be here, Unc." I could hear Kenny struggling, like he was pushing against something or someone.

"Nah, fuck that. Fuck them police. They don't run shit over here. I just wanna come in and talk to you."

"Unc, it's 9 in the morning. You smell like liquor. Just, can we go by Uncle Bray's house and everyone can talk there?

"I said I'm coming inside motherfucka," his uncle's voice slurred and the *thud* of a body hitting the tile floor made me jump. I put a hand on the doorknob, ready to run to Kenny's aide, but paused to hear his voice say, "Unc, be careful. C'mon, man, get up. You can't be here. C'mon." He wasn't the one who fell.

"Fuck you, lil nigga. It's your fault. Fuck you!"

"Unc, I can't do this right now," Kenny's voice thickened. The subject matter was a lot on him and his uncle had shown up, abruptly shoving him right back into that nightmare. I looked to my phone, wondering if it were my place to turn it on and call the police.

"Boy my son is gone 'cuz of you! Hear me? Gone!"

"Unc! Whoa! Wait a minute! Fuck–wait–Ay, WAIT!" A scuffle had ensued, and Kenny released a dreadful "Aahk!" That was it.

I hopped over to his closet and found my courage to go out and help him. I raced into his living room, gun pointed, but looked down and dropped it immediately. It landed with a *clack* as my quivering fingers scraped down my face. "Uh-AAAAHHHHHHHH!" I screamed at the top of my vocal register. "AHHHH!!!" I dropped down to my knees.

Kenny was shuddering on the floor in a growing pool of his own blood. It spouted from his neck. Diamond droplets accumulated in his ears. His eyes begged for my help as he lay gurgling, spitting, and choking blood.

"No no no no no no! Kenny, hold on! Kenny!" His body continued to jerk and I held my hands down over his, clutching his neck wound, although it served none to keep the rhythmic spurt from pouring through our fingers. "Oh my GOD!" I applied pressure and looked to his uncle, who'd been backing outside one exaggerated step at a time. A neighbor sprinted up to the doorway in a bathrobe, and stumbled backward at the scene.

"Call an ambulance!" I screamed. A switchblade dropped from his uncle's fingers and he turned to run, tripping and falling over the paralyzed neighbor. He picked himself up clumsily and got a running start low from the ground, although as soon as he ran out of view, I could hear him shout, "Got damn!" and the thump of his body into the grass.

"Get help!" I screamed once more. "Help, please!"

Kenny's body had stopped shuddering already. I squeezed my eyes shut and flung my head side to side. "No! Nonononono. Kenny you better not! Stay with me PLEASE! Baby!" I glanced down. He was stuck in a permanent, unblinking gaze, head down on its side. Arms limp. No gurgles. No breathing. No pulse. "Noooooo," I bellowed, and let my head fall into his chest. I beat on his belly and sat upright, taking his head in my hands. Forehead to forehead I howled, "Get up, Kennyyyyy, oh my God!"

But Kenny did not get up. He did not blink or shut his silver eyes. Kneeling in his blood, I bawled and continued to try and revive him.

46

The detective's request to reduce my charges worked beautifully in my favor. I still had charges, but with the nature of the murder charge being lessened, in addition to one count versus two, the judge determined a bail amount of $45,000 instead of two hundred thousand. He'd literally said that at the arraignment. He said that clearly they'd gotten some of the initial facts about the incident wrong and that further investigation was due before they could formally charge me with first-degree murder, and that for the time being, manslaughter was it.

I had rejected another bogus ass public defender who'd come in spitting more bullshit, deciding I'd select an attorney to my liking once I was freed from holding. I stood before the judge, temporarily representing myself, and pleaded not-guilty. The judge signaled for that motion to be filed and then acknowledged that the murder investigation itself would take months before the trial could receive a date. Even a preliminary hearing was now going to take a hot minute. I was given the opportunity to contact someone and explain the terms of my bail. I wasn't trying to rot behind bars, waiting for them to figure the shit out.

I damn sure had some things to see to on the outside.

I was too hot right now so I could forget about trying to get my supply man to front me. I contacted Shakima, who was realistically my only resort. Shakima, for my son's sake, was the only one who had access to my secret stash, although she didn't know it.

She was silent at first following the automated voice which notified her that the call was being recorded by the county. I started first. "Shakima?"

"Dash? Shit…," she sucked her teeth. "Don't pull me into no shit you got goin' on. I'm not interested."

"Kima don't fuckin' hang up. Yeah, I'm doing great thanks for fucking asking."

"Where are you calling me from? I can't help you."

"Actually you can. I need you to bring my bail money to the court."

"What? You lost yo' fucking mind? I'm not touching your dirty money and bringing it no fucking where."

"Kima could you watch your goddamn mouth on this line? What the fuck you tryna do?"

"Mm mm. Call your bitch."

"This is *not* the time for that, yo. I need a favor and you're the only one that can get it done for me."

"I ain't puttin' up no fucking money for you, I ain't putting up my house for you, my car for you, nothing."

"That raggedy ass whip you pushin' ain't 'bout to help nothing shake. Be serious. Listen, I don't need none of that. Just go to the Wells Fargo by Cumberland Mall. It's a big ass one you can't miss. I got a safety deposit box there. Listen, you can't get into it yourself, but I got a banker there by the name of Price Varner. Request to speak to him, and give him our son's middle name, birthday, and social, plus the words "banana farm." Aight?"

"Uh…what?"

"It's stupid, yes I know. It's the safe word. He'll know it's serious and that I specifically sent you. Have him contact the court, and everything will get worked out from there. That's your only part in it. I promise."

Shakima's attitude blew static over our connection and she sucked her teeth. "I just got to work, asshole."

"Kima, this is important. I *need* this from you. How the fuck else I'ma keep you paid up each month if I'm in here." There was no initial response from her. Check mate. She sighed again and told me to hold while she grabbed a pen.

"Got me pressed like I'm bout to remember all this bullshit. Say all that again."

I took a deep breath and relaxed a little, knowing that if she followed my instructions just right, I'd be out by the evening.

A quarter after seven PM, Shakima's Kia came into view, and I stepped out the courthouse doors, newly released and free to go. I spun to check the backseat as soon as I sat into the passenger side. The car seat was empty. I knew just then how this was going to go down. Per my request, Kima brought me to my place. She had little to say to me for the entire car ride, and after she pulled up, she unlocked the doors and mumbled, "You welcome, by the way. Bye, nigga."

"Where's Quan. By your mother?"

She rolled her eyes. "Yes, Dash. Obviously."

"Well can you bring me over there to see him?"

She looked at me like I'd just asked her to drive us off a cliff. "You fucking kidding, right? You just got out of jail. You think my family *hasn't* heard that you killed some niggas? You think they want you around Quan? You think *I* want you 'round Quan? Uh uh, that's cap."

"Kima, Quan is my son. The last few days been hard enough. What you think I been thinkin' bout this whole time? It ain't my fault you *didn't* bring my son to see his Daddy. You think after all this bullshit that he not the first person I wanted to see? You don't know shit about what happened, so I could give a fuck what you or your mother feel about it, either way."

Kima looked at me, long and hard.

"I won't disrespect your mother or her house. I'll sit in the car. Just bring him out to the car and let me lay my eyes on him. I'll tell him everything is okay. Shit, we can go to eat as a lil *family,"* I huffed, emphasizing the word with air quotes. "Then ya'll can drop me right back here and I'll be out your way for a minute. That's what you want and that's what you'll get."

Again, Kima didn't move for a while, she just stared at me. The suspense she created had my teeth on edge. I was running out of the patience required to keep this act believable. Finally, she rolled her eyes and put the car in park. "Go brush your teeth or something. Ya' breath smell like ass."

"Give me ten minutes," I promised, and hopped out, jogging to my door as she rolled up to park. I opened the door to my condo with little effort, since the shit was unlocked, probably since the police ran through it. It was pretty obvious that they'd been there. All my shit was emptied out all over the place. I expected that. They'd probably broke in that day before they found me, thinking that I'd be holed up in here instead of on the run like any other sane individual. Didn't matter or affect my plan.

I brushed my teeth and washed my face in record time, and changed into new basketball shorts and a fresh tee. I went into the secret compartment under my bathroom sink and removed a small revolver gun and its ammo. Once properly loaded, I shoved it down into my basketball shorts and went back outside. Didn't need my house key or wallet, so fuck it.

I hopped back in Shakima's whip and brought the gun out of my pocket as soon as she switched into reverse. She didn't notice what I had in my hand until I stuck it down into her hip. She looked down, did a double-take and screamed. "Dash, what the fuck!"

"I'm not going to do anything to you as long as I don't have to. It's simple. We're going where I tell you and that's it."

"I'll take you to him! I told you that! Are you crazy!"

"Yes. We not going to Quan. We going to Clarkston. Drive. I'll tell you where to go."

Shakima sat perfectly upright with both hands on the wheel and started to cry. "Dash," she sobbed. "Why are you doin' this?"

"Because they took my whip and my phone. I said, drive. That's all I need you to do."

47

Dougie slowed the truck as we approached my building. He rolled around alongside my walkway, and pulled up behind a Kia that sat in wait with its lights off, probably waiting for someone to come out.

"I can't come inside tonight. I gotta hit my next stop, bae. Unless you need me," Dougie smirked.

"I think I'm good," I cheesed. "I'll be ready. Or if you wanna get breakfast first you can come a lil earlier and I can –," my suggestion was interrupted by a blunt thump on Dougie's side. I looked up and my head flew back. I must've been seeing things. Dougie's hand was already sliding down into the car door's pocket. I knew what he had down there. "Sunshine. Get out the car slow. Right now."

Dash tapped Dougie's driver's side again one time, with the butt of his gun, same as he'd just done. "Step out the car, fuck nigga." I was froze. The Kia's lights flicked on and it sped off and flung out into traffic.

"Sunshine, get out. Don't go around. Just get out and get low."

I undid my lock and pulled the lever to let myself out. Against Dougie's advice, I shuffled around the front of the truck. Holding my hands out, I approached my baby daddy. "Dash, what are you doing? How'd you…,"

"What. How'd I get out? Or how'd I know you was riding with this fuck nigga behind my back? Man, I knew you been fuckin' this nigga" Dash cocked his gun, icing me in my tracks. The muzzle of Dougie's Tec-9 appeared over the lowering sheet of glass.

"Point it at her and it's your brain on the pavement, nigga." My heart throbbed against my tonsils. I was breathing like I'd just run a lap of the lot.

"Ya'll, please." I begged. "Not this, ya'll. Please."

"I ain't fuckin' round wit'cha, boy." Dougie stated, disregarding me altogether. Dash hadn't raised his gun, but didn't take his finger off the trigger, either. He faced me, turned his eyes to Dougie from their corners, and then focused on me again, shaking his head. "Nah, you did this, bitch. Don't beg me now. You can fuck 'round 'n have this nigga. But he *not* bout to be raisin' my seed. Did she tell you that, nigga? Bet you ain't know that shit," Dash smiled, turning his head to Dougie in hopes of catching a satisfying glimpse of Dougie's confusion. Instead Dougie laughed at him.

"She's ten weeks and five days. Next."

Dash boiled over and lifted his free hand to his head. "Oh shit," he mumbled. And then louder. "Oh shit! I was right! The baby isn't mine? Is it!"

I dropped down into a squat, seemingly my go-to when enough was enough. I brought both hands up and covered my eyes for a second.

"Ay, bitch!" I heard, but before I even opened my eyes all the way, rapid shots pierced the air, followed by one booming pop. The scream in the background was coming from my mouth, and I fell back onto my butt, scrambling backward, continuing to scream at the sight of Dash laying motionless on the ground.

"Sunshine…Sunshine!" I heard Dougie's voice faintly call. My head spun up, instantly blinded by the Tahoe's halogen beamers. "Sunshine," Dougie was still calling for me. The realization that he could've been injured or worse hit me and I shot up to my feet the same instant. In three wide steps I was close enough to see him sitting with his head pressed against the seat, gripping his collarbone. His breathing was uneven. Dash was behind my feet, and I was trying my best not to look down. I covered my mouth and squeezed my eyes shut, unable to let my mind grasp this as reality. I had to be stuck in a terrible nightmare. I just needed to wake up.

Doors in the two adjacent buildings were being opened and slammed shut, and I knew sirens would be coming around the corner any minute. Still, I refused to look down to the ground.

Dougie continued to wheeze and said, "Sunshine. Go inside. When the cops get here. Make sure you're inside."

"Dougie…" Tears buried whatever else I thought I had to say.

"Go inside, Sun…Sunshine. I'ma be aight. That nigga not. I'm okay. Just hurts. Go, now."

I nodded, and just then, fingers loosely gripped my ankle. I yelped and hopped away. Dash had managed to bring one arm up over his head and when I hopped out of his reach, his body went limp, and he exhaled a long, trailing breath. I stepped up to him, both hands to my mouth, and broke down. I knew immediately that I'd never think of him from that moment forth without seeing exactly this, Dash lying motionless in a puddle of blood, his shirt soaked red, with one arm raised to ask an eternity of questions. "Dash," I whined his name, one last time.

"Sunshine," Dougie called my name urgently. I snapped out of it and returned to my side of the car to retrieve my purse and phone. "Go," Dougie said as I gripped the door to shut it. "I'm sorry, Sunshine. He was coming for you. I reacted. I'm sorry."

I took his apology and sprinted up the stairs for my apartment. The sirens were finally approaching. I dumped the contents of my wallet out on my living room floor and jittery hands pulled out Detective Beverly's card. I grabbed for my phone. I had to get her on the line as soon as possible.

48

I'd gone through half a roll of toilet paper by the time Detective Beverly arrived. I sat on my couch wrapped in a blanket, bawling my eyes out, different police in and out of my door, once again. This time they weren't trashing the place or knocking in doors; just trying to get me calm enough to talk. I told them I'd talk to Detective Beverly only, and most of them got out of my face after that except for one pushy officer who tried to come off like he wasn't applying pressure, but he was.

Detective Beverly stepped inside, hands in the pockets of a gray zip-up windbreaker. She gave the bulky, ashy officer a look that couldn't be confused. He had a black mother, and so he knew it well. He nodded to her, and exited the apartment. Detective Beverly leaned up against the wall near the kitchen entrance and took her hands out, rubbing them up and down her sides. "It's getting nippy at night."

I sniffled and blew my nose. She held her lips in and waited on me to start talking. "Thank you for coming. I didn't know who else to call," I managed to say before breaking down again. Blue and red police lights still bounced off the walls in striped splotches. With the front door closed, it served as the only illumination carving Detective Beverly out from the dark.

"Can we turn the lights on in here?" she asked.

"I don't want the lights on," I replied. I don't know why. I just didn't. She reached around the wall and lit the kitchen, anyway, turning back to me with an unapologetic face.

"I'm a little irritated with this whole situation, Tonnie. A lot more disappointed in you."

"Me? What did I –,"

"The last time we spoke you agreed you'd do better for yourself. Your child," she interjected, holding out a single hand, gesturing downward toward my stomach. "You ran right back into the streets? You said you had a legitimate job lined up. You were going to spend more time with your sister. Look after her. Maybe keep her away from making the same mistakes you're still making with that drug dealing boyfriend she has."

My eyes widened. I'd never told her that last bit. She marked my cognition and smirked. "I'm not a detective for nothing, Tonnie. Come on, now."

"I did start my job," I decided to address instead. "Everything was going so good. This week was perfect."

"And this new boyfriend? By perfect you mean opening up designer bags you can't afford filled with drug money?" I stared at her, doe-eyed again. She was good. Then again, that video had gone up for all the public to see. Last time I looked at my page it was at 28.6k views. I didn't think that the cops were paying attention to me or even that someone at a desk somewhere was watching my moves like that.

"Detective, it wasn't going to happen overnight. I got bills. The streets know me. It's how I eat. I didn't know that nigga Dash," I paused and corrected myself. "I didn't expect him to pop up and do this."

At the mention of him, she scoffed and gave an exaggerated eye roll to the ceiling. "Oh no, he's definitely a moron. I put my name on the line for him and now someone's going to have my ass." She blew a hard breath through her nostrils and closed her eyes, saying, "sorry about your loss," without attempting to hide her reluctance at all.

"I wanted to be the one to tell you that it was Dash. It was *all* him. Dougie wasn't doing anything but tryna drop me home from work. He was defending me. Dash surprised us in the parking lot. He had a gun, he rolled up on us, and I ain't know *what* he was planning to do."

Detective brought a notepad up from her back pocket and flipped it open. "Tonnie, slow it down."

I nodded and took a deep breath. "Dougie didn't do anything but try to protect me is what I'm tryna tell you. Dash must've got out somehow and heard that I was talkin' to someone new and when I got out the car he pulled a gun on me. He was just trying to protect me, I swear. Please. I don't want him to go away, too. I swear to you it wasn't his fault." I was pleading so hard I was hiccupping over each and every word, snot-nosed crying.

"Now when you say 'he' and 'Dougie', that's the nickname for the shooter, correct?"

I sputtered, coming to realize I had no idea what Dougie's real name was. Not any part of it, nor where the name "Dougie" originated from. I didn't want to agree that he was *the shooter*, either. He was *the defender* in my eyes. "He protected me. I don't know what Dash had on his mind but he had a gun and Dougie put him down. He was not 'bout to let him come at me. He saved my life," I said, my reverence for him coming through in my voice. "Is he okay?"

Detective Beverly looked up from writing and paused. She seemed conflicted to say so, but nodded. "He'll make it."

The relief that washed over me was indescribable. I buried my face in more tissues and let that tension go, one sob at a time.

49

I was supposed to be packing up my things. I'd started emptying my dresser into a duffel bag, and that was as far as I got before Muni Long's Time Machine lyrics truly resonated with me. Since the first two minutes after I'd started, I was spread across the carpet, staring up with the most neutral expression, crying a stream of tears into my ears. I didn't have any energy left to participate in the act of bawling or weeping. I'd been doing that non-stop over the past week. In front of everyone. The police, detectives, my parents, Tonnie, Porsha, Kenny's mom, my academic head. I was surprised I had tears left to cry at all.

By the time the song was on its fourth replay, Tonnie crashed in, desperately searching for my phone. She gave up and resorted to simply shutting down the baby blue JBL speaker sitting on my windowsill. After Muni's voice was abruptly cut, Tonnie came over and stood over me.

"I asked for space, Tonnie." I said flatly, my eyes still fixed on the ceiling fan.

"Okay and I get that but I'm not going to let you downright torture yourself. I just paid attention to the words. Not that song on repeat. No."

"Why not. At least someone out there understands."

Tonnie sighed and got down to her knees. "Ginger," she said. I wouldn't look at her so she got all the way down and laid out next to me. We were both on our backs, quiet for a couple of minutes.

"Reggie is gonna be here in the morning. You can't ask for space and then not get stuff done. I know it hurts. I know."

"Do you? Your boyfriend is still alive, at least." It wasn't the fairest thing to say, but it's what came out first. I didn't exactly know how Tonnie felt about Dash's death. She hadn't expressed it around me and I didn't ask. Still, the depth of the silence pressing us into the floor after my comment carried in it a deep pain, and Tonnie sniffled. "I'm sorry," I mumbled, still unable to turn and look.

"You know," she sniffed again. "At my first appointment the doctor had said somethin' like I'm not gonna be able to feel the baby move or kick or none a' that at least until like month four or five. Yet here I am almost three months, and I feel it. Not any hard kicks or nothin' crazy but every now and then I feel flutters and it catches me off guard." She released the half-hearted beginning of a laugh and continued. "That's when it's the hardest. That's when I can't ignore that last image I have of Dash. And then it takes a minute before I can *not* see it. You know? Yeah…It's all I can see for a while sometimes. You're not alone, Ginger. It's all I want you to know."

I swallowed back the urge to break, and finally looked at Tonnie, whose face was contorting as she fought the same battle. I reached over and took her hand off her chest, and then switched it to my closer hand. She squeezed, and I turned back to the ceiling fan, choosing to stay strong for her this time.

At some point we'd gotten up off the floor and Tonnie changed my playlist entirely before she began helping me pack. I wasn't aware of the time nor had I even looked at my phone to know how much time had passed, but before I knew it, all my suitcases were full, and we'd moved into my bathroom, placing my stuff into a small Home Depot box along with my belongings from the hallways linen closet. That's when Tonnie announced that she was hungry. I wasn't, so I just kept packing. Before I knew it, she was accepting a pizza at the door and had called me out to join her.

"Not hungry!" I called back. Just as I knew she would, Tonnie came back into my room and shot me a commanding look.

"You not 'bout to starve on my watch. Just come and try. Please?" Reluctant, I gave in and met her in the living room. The pizza box and a one liter soda was on the coffee table. Same time I knelt down, Fran stepped out of her bedroom door, locked it, and turned her nose up as she crossed the room. "Bitch, keep on then," Tonnie snapped, and then stared Fran down the entire time, daring her to say something or even look back.

Fran picked up her pace a little and then slammed the front door shut behind herself. Tonnie stuck her neck out and rolled her eyes. "Bitches got real problems," she huffed.

"Oh, I know. I never fucked with her like that."

We both took bites into our slices. I didn't think that I wanted to eat at first, but the smell coaxed me into it. The sound that jumped from my stomach the moment the first bite went down halted both of us. I envisioned a chewed lump of food hitting a lake of sulfuric acid, sizzling and sinking slowly. Tonnie shook her head. "Mm hmm."

I grinned and poured myself some Coke. I cleared my throat, sipped, and watched my sister thumb through her TikTok feed. She seemed stable enough for me to ask. "How's he doing, anyway. Just curious."

She'd offered most of my emotional support in the week since our incidents. When we were on the carpet together earlier, I realized just how absorbed in Kenny's loss that I've been, treating it like it was the worst loss between the two of us. Or maybe, treating her like she had a duty to care for me more than for herself as the big sister. It was selfish of me, either way.

Tonnie broke her attention away from her phone and put up a half-grin. "He's recovered for the most part. Yesterday he said he can move his arm up and down a lil bit without it killing him. Taking the pain pills less often. I know he hate them shits."

"They still won't consider letting him post a bail?"

Her head swung side to side and she sipped her cup, jumping her eyebrows in anticipation of her own words. "Nope." She belched. "Dash pretty much fucked that up for him with this whole case. No one is willing to put themselves on the line for a nigga. Detective Beverly understands how it all went down but she isn't willing to bother the DA again. She said she already knows what they'll say."

I sighed. "Damn." Tonnie nodded and kept eating. "Yup," she agreed between bites.

Aside from the sound of our eating, silence ensued. I put my half-eaten slice down, finished with it altogether, and took a seat at the back row of my thoughts. Eventually, I was the one to speak next. "You know, I still can't believe how crazy it is that everything we went through mirrored each other the way it did."

She swallowed the first bite of her second slice and nodded, "That part."

"You think that somehow everything happened like that for a reason?" She heard how frail my voice had become, and paused from chewing to look at me. All I could think about was how I'd turned my phone off and couldn't answer her calls when she needed me, and by the time Kenny was being carried away underneath a white sheet, Tonnie's phone was put on silent and she'd gone to sleep. Similar to the day we were both arrested. As our lives were mimicking one another's at the same times of the same days, we were unable to show up for each other when we needed it most. We each had to handle our own shit in those moments, unavailable despite our struggles being nearly identical.

"No, Ginger. Not at all. Don't overthink it. Life just be like that. Fucking crazy," she shrugged, dismissing it. I knew she wasn't giving it as deep of a thought as I was, nor was she thinking in the same direction. Instead of spelling it out or trying to get her to see what I meant, I shrugged, too, and brought my napkin up to dot my eyes dry. I poured myself more soda.

Tonnie burped again. "So Bethune, huh?"

"Yea. Well, for the Spring. Not right now. I'm gonna spend some time at home for a while. Try to forget that this all happened."

"I feel you."

"Yeah." I let out a burp of my own and stood to throw out my paper plate. Dad had really pushed for UNF, saying he'd already had the necessary conversations to make the transition easy, but I declined. Nothing about Jacksonville appealed to me. What stuck with me, however, was the campus tour I'd taken at Bethune-Cookman during my senior year. Back then I'd told myself it would be my next pick if Clark Atlanta rejected me. Thankfully, that wasn't the case.

Come to think of it, these days, after everything, I wasn't exactly sure I could say that I was thankful. Atlanta had chewed me to the bone and spit me out, bare.

50

Two months and a half after the night Dash was shot and killed, I'd finally learned Dougie's full name at his preliminary hearing. Zayvion Dernell Jules–Walker. While it was a mouthful, I must say, I loved it more than the nickname. Had me wondering where the hell "Dougie" had even come from. I didn't even wanna call him that anymore.

At his hearing, his lawyer explained to the courtroom that the gun was lawfully registered to him and therefore not illegal, any proposed drug charges would not successfully stick due to lack of evidence, and that the investigation had thus far already proven that Dash was depraved of mind, armed, and dangerous. Apparently, because he was in his car when Dash approached and he never got out, Dougie's lawyer persuaded the judge that the state of Georgia wouldn't be able to successfully prosecute against Stand Your Ground law. He called Dougie's innocence a "no-brainer". Dougie's lawyer stood up, held his hand down toward Dougie, and told the judge, "what you see here, your honor, is a hero. And so will a jury of his peers." All of this agreed, the judge announced that taking this case to trial would be a waste of tax dollars, declared Dougie's time in holding as time served, and slammed his gavel. Court adjourned. Dougie was a free man!

Dougie stood, holding up triumphant fists. I stepped around the banister separating us and flung my arms around his neck. I fell into him, sobbing. A bailiff stepped up and waited for me to let go so that he could release Dougie's wrists. Once the cuffs were removed, Dougie grabbed me up onto my tiptoes and kissed my face over and over again. We pulled each other in and rocked side to side. I couldn't stop the tears from flowing.

We turned to leave the courtroom with his lawyer, and I'd caught a glimpse of Detective Beverly seated in the second to last row. She nodded to me and held up a sideways fist. She shook it once and held it there in support of our win. I nodded my head and pulled my lips in, thankful to have her on our side. She was literally seated on our side, after all.

That night, we went back to Strokers to celebrate. I didn't feel a way about it. It would forever be a special place to us. It was where we first met. His guys were glad to have their main man back on deck. He deserved that love.

I'd put on something extra classy. I wore chocolate colored Salone Monet pumps with a long burgundy, high-slit velvet dress. It hugged my curves immaculately – including my bump. I was showing now, just enough for everyone to know for sure it was a baby and not an extra plate. I wore my hair down, ironed out bone straight, parted down the middle. With my Celine over my shoulder, we walked in together hand in hand. The DJ stopped the music.

"Oh shit!" The DJ sounded the fog horn alert multiple times before letting the sound effect play out. The instrumental to Lil Will's song of the same name began to play. "It's the man himself! The king of the hustle! The Robin Hood of the Hood! Atlanta's dope boy of the year! I call him Jacquees big brother! Fuckin' wit'cha man. Dougie is IN the BUILDING! Yuh!" The DJ sped through that introduction and then Dougie's music faded.

A short gap of silence followed. Then, all throughout the club, a woman's voice filled the air, saying, "I have got a girl who's pussy is so good, if you threw it up in the air, it would turn into Sunshine." I pulled my lip in and turned to Dougie, squeezing his hand gently. I used to start my sets with that clip from Harlem Nights every time I hit the main stage. A smile budded on his lips and he tilted his head to the side and said, "no cap". The DJ continued.

"On his arm is one of the baddest to do it! The diamond princess! A-Town Barbie! Dummy thick wit' it! She fell in love with the plug ya'll. You know you stalkin' her Instagram page, right NOW! I know I am! The hood celebrity. Her highness. In the flesh. Stroker's very own, Sunshiiiiine!" The DJ spun down a record, and the bass of Normani's Wild Side dropped. Whole time, I was giggling, waving off the DJ's words. Then I stuck out my tongue and started to point everyone's attention back to Dougie. He tugged my hand and brought his face down, licked his lips, and we kissed in front of everyone, full tongue. The club went up! Swear it felt like we'd just got married or some shit. It was the best feeling.

We were seated at a VIP table, surrounded by his boys and thirsty ass dancers. His guys were truly showing out tonight. Seemed like every dancer who wasn't on stage was trying to find a spot to shake they ass in our section. Especially after Bright stepped back and threw a wad of cash in the air. It rained down on Dougie and I, and Bright hollered, "My boy beat the case! Yerrrrr!" Red had the nerve to come and try to dance in the center of the money rain, and turned her jiggly ass toward Dougie. Dougie turned to me and grabbed my hips, pulled me up, and sat me right in his lap. Everyone who saw him do that began laughing, and Red got lost, as she should have.

When another one of his homie's popped a bottle of champagne in our section, Dougie poured his plastic cup full and held it up to toast, and then caught himself, busting out laughing. I tried my best to keep a straight face as he cleared his throat and said, "my fault, my fault." He reached over to the ice bucket, putting a few cubes in a second plastic cup. He grabbed up a mini water bottle and cracked it open. After handing me my ice water, Dougie held up his champagne cup again. We tapped cups and drank up, and he pinched my chin as I finished.

Afterward, Dougie brought me back to his high-rise apartment. All of this time had passed, and it was my first time there. I stepped out onto his balcony and took in the view. It was beautiful. All of Downtown Atlanta glittered against the moonlit sky. Dougie came up behind to embrace me, resting his chin on my shoulder. "It's nice, huh."

"It's gorgeous."

"I know…" he whispered. "She is."

I turned to him. He took both my hands between his fingers and nudged his chin up, gazing beyond me. "You can walk out every night and see it just like this, whenever you're ready."

I didn't even know what to say to that. Dougie had become a blessing to my life in more ways than one, and right on time. He sensed that I was a little overwhelmed, and looked down, embarrassed. I stepped in and kissed his neck. We met lips, sharing a long, tender kiss. We were back inside on his plush L-shaped sofa by time either one of us had come up for air. Dougie unbuttoned the top of my dress at the nape of my neck, and I kicked off my shoes and straddled him. I helped him remove his glasses and his shirt. He threw them aside and kicked his sneakers off as well. We continued to help each other undress and Dougie ran his hands up and down my bare skin, looking up at me and shaking his head slow. "We was just like this the moment I first fell in love with you, girl."

I blushed. "We…what?" I was caught up in a euphoric bliss. I wanted to hear him say it again.

"Oh yeah." He nodded. "The second time I ever saw you on stage I told my boy, *that's the one.* Niggas laughed at me n' shit. I know. I was trippin'. But I had to get you. I knew I had to get you. That was the first time I paid you for a private dance."

"I do remember our first private session."

"Shit, I ain't *ever* forget. We was just like this. I think…I think Girls Need Love was playing and you was on my lap stretched across me. I wanted to fuck the sense outta you."

I giggled. "Oh yeah?"

"Hell yeah," he smiled. "It was more than that, though. I got to really look in your eyes. The shit was instant. A nigga fell for you, ma."

"All that time?"

"All that time. I found out who you was with and I had to check myself, granted. But I made sure I showed you as much love as possible every time, just in case."

"So that's why, huh?"

"Yeah. That's why." Dougie was still rubbing my thighs in circles, and his erection prodded up into the crotch of my thong panties. He leaned up and bit my shoulder, allowing his tongue to linger over my skin. My eyes rolled back. He sat back again and watched me enjoy his attention. Another smile budded. "I feel like I defeated the entire world. That's how I know you really a queen. You make a nigga feel like I'm the king of the city."

I smirked. "Is that the Moet talking?"

He blushed and turned his head, "Nah, man. Stop playin'. I'm bein' for real." He sized me up in his lap and released an "Mm". He continued massaging my cheeks. "I missed you."

"I came to see you like every other day."

"I know. Thank you."

"You welcome, baby," I kissed him.

"Oh, we're going to go get your car tomorrow. Almost forgot about that," Dougie said. It was an awkward time to bring it up, but I could tell that it had genuinely just popped up in his mind. During visitations he'd explained that he'd bought me a BMW in cash, lessening the chance that it would be seized by law enforcement if they decided to play dirty. However, I couldn't just walk in and get it without him since he'd put his name on the title and not mine. Unfortunately it was sitting there with a bow on it, waiting to be claimed this entire time.

That reminded me. "So, this whole time I'm calling you Dougie. Never mind that you have a beautiful first name. Zayvion?"

Dougie chuckled and shook his head. "Quit playin'." He was blushing harder than me now.

"I'm serious. How'd Dougie come from that?"

"It didn't. Don't laugh. I'ma tell you, but you can't laugh, aight?"

"I swear."

"Aight. My nickname been Dougie since my freshman year at college." My brows went up. I was surprised he went to college. I didn't see that coming. He read my face and added, "I went to Morehouse for one year. Dropped out. But I was at an Iota party, and I won a dougie contest. Everyone on campus started calling me Dougie." We fell over laughing. "Man, you promised."

"Sorry, sorry. Forgive me. But from now on, I'm calling you Zay."

Zay looked up into my eyes solemnly and nodded. "Yes ma'am. Even though…," He brought both hands up behind my neck and began leaning me back, bearing my weight in his arms as he leaned forward. "Only my family calls me that." Zay kissed my belly softly, and looked up into my eyes. I shivered and melted to his whim.

Zay picked me up as he stood, my legs perfectly wrapped around his waist, and carried me into his bedroom. He placed me on his bed, took off my thong, and parted my legs. He brought his face down into my neck and traced his lips down and around my chest. Our thick breathing filled the room, and he paused to remove his draws. Gently as ever, Zay positioned and entered my body.

We moaned, panted, whined, and grinded together, holding nothing back, until the sun's first light brought in a new day.

www.ingramcontent.com/pod-product-compliance
Lightning Source LLC
La Vergne TN
LVHW010550160826
845677LV00013B/3073

* 9 7 9 8 3 5 8 2 5 5 1 6 6 *